OUT 4 $ELF

ANOTHER HOOD TALE
BY
MS. MICHEL MOORE

OUT 4 $ELF

If this book was purchased without a cover on it please be aware that neither the Author nor the Publisher has received payment and you know that crap ain't right!

OUT 4 $ELF© 2006 Michel Moore

All rights reserved. Be advised that no part of this book may be reproduced, stored in or introduced into a retrieval system or transmitted in any form, electronic, mechanical, photocopying or otherwise without written permission from the publisher.

First Print- June 2007

ISBN-978-0-9759991-3-3

ISBN- 0-9769991-3-7

LCCN-

Say U Promise Publications
　PO.Box 38162
Detroit, Michigan 48238

　www.sayupromise.com

This novel is a work of fiction. It is not meant to portray or depict ant real persons, living or dead. Any references to locales and events are a product of the Ms. Moore's vivid and colorful imagination.

Cover Design: MS GRAPHICS/ Marcus Margerum
Photos: Diamond Pix/ Sean Darnell

Models: Master D.J. Lorrick
　　　　BAILEY-　www.myspace.com
　　　　　　　　/BAILEYSANDCREAM

MS. MICHEL MOORE

THE WORD ON THE STREETS

"My girl Michel has proven to be amongst the elite of Motown's rising stars."

-K'wan,- National best selling author of Gangsta, Eve, Street Dreams, Hoodlum, Hood Rat and Road Dawg.

"Rough, Raw in ya face Reality! Damn Michel! Do ya thang and make it rain on Detroit and the entire Urban Lit Game."

-Valencia Williams-Essence Magazine Bestselling author of The Hottest Summer Ever Known and Vindictive Women.

"Michel Moore shares an urban tale that rocks neighborhoods worldwide introducing readers to the real ghetto experience."

-T.C.Littles -author of Knowledge Costs

"This blazin' hot page turner will have ya fingertips on fire!"

-Deanna Michelle Smith, author of Reign Storm and Outlaw City

"OUT 4 $ELF...is an eviction notice for all street lit authors not keeping it real. Ya time is up!"

-Othello Lewis Sr.-book vendor, Brooklyn, NY.

MS. MICHEL MOORE

OUT 4 $ELF

~DEDICATION~

TO EACH AND EVERY PERSON IN THE

LINWOOD/DEXTER/DAVISON AREA

THE STRUGGLE CONTINUES…

MS. MICHEL MOORE

OUT 4 $ELF

RESPECT DUE

First The Almighty Creator, who knows my heart, I give unconditionally my praise.

John, where do I begin? What the hell can I say? I love ya Good Country Ass!

Ma, you always speak your mind, even when a chick ain't trying to hear it.

Damn Tiffany! U made it back! Mad love 2 my first born!

My little sister Fleasha, we didn't have to send ole boy on vacation this time to make shit happen.

Dwayne Fletcher, my big brother, the ultimate peacekeeper in the family.
♥ Mr. Jayden James Warren, my new little man.♥
My girl Kim Mc Laurin, the only true hustler from back in the day I run with. Point Blank!

All the chicks reppin' 'THE D'- Dortheia, Paulette, Jazmine, Chari, Kenyel, My girl Kenya(B-ware of the problem solvers) Yolanda(girl ya ass be there every Friday) Detroit's Top Notch Players- Sanford, Byron, Marlon and Christopher Tatum the puppet master to the game and 'O' who gave me encouragement when I really needed it. Jonathon Edison, the best motivational speaker on the planet, you're an inspiration to me.

Bernard, my friend who keeps me from going freaking insane.

MS. MICHEL MOORE

OUT 4 SELF

My daughter Charday, who graces the hot ass cover of all my other novels, I love Ya!

Marcus Margerum, my brother from another mother…Holler at him. He's definitely the best graphic artist around.

My Folks holding Glendale down 4 life- Mark Gardener, Kenneth Young, Brandon Foy(Say U Promise), Tim Reeves

Tasia, my family over at MLK High School, mad respect for holding things down when a chick can't.

Diane- Come back we all miss you!

Peace to all my little cousins- Sherra, Jr., Tenera, CoCo, Moosie, Lil Mike, Liza, BooBoo, Mark, Chyna, Toni and Tonya.

That Alabama Love- La Rosia, Mance, Sonya, Ava, Helen, Molly, Mike, Maine, Cat, Sable and the rest of my Fam.

Everyone over at Magicians Ink- Icing out the bling on the personalized jerseys- You Know How We Do!

Neasha Lorrick, thanks for loaning your handsome son to the world. Now everyone sees just how cute he is!

Urban Book Source, Virgo, Green, Lady Scorpio, Le-Le and Hotcokle. Oh hell, the entire family of Coast2Coast Readers.

Special words of <u>Respect, Loyalty</u> and <u>Gratitude</u> goes to one of the most hard working men in the Literary World that took a chance on a sister, going the extra mile. Thank You a million times over <u>Bro. Nati</u> and everyone at <u>Afrikan World Books</u>.

MS. MICHEL MOORE

OUT 4 $ELF

IDUSTRY TALK

First to all the African American Bookstores that show a chick mad love, I appreciate you humbly and tip my hat to you! <u>Source Of Knowledge</u> in Newark, <u>The Truth</u> representing Southfield, <u>Tiffany</u> holding things down for a sister in <u>Jayden's Joint</u>, <u>Shrine Of The Black Madonna</u> Bookstore still standing strong 35 years and counting, <u>Hood Book Headquarters</u> in Warren, my friend <u>TRU</u> at <u>Tru Books</u> in Connecticut and Stephanie at <u>Urban Knowledge</u> reppin' Baltimore. Special love to <u>Hakim</u> doing the damn thang in Philly at his spot <u>Black and Nobel Books</u>. <u>Kevon</u> in Brooklyn, <u>Ice</u> over at <u>Harlem World</u> and <u>Wes Beatty</u> at <u>Digital Data</u>.

ALL THE GREAT AUTHORS IN THE TRENCHES MAKING THAT SHIT HAPPEN IN DETROIT

Deanna Smith, AVN, Contel Bradford, Erica Martin, Dex Michael Lee, Sylvia Hubbard, Dennis Reed, Janaya Black E. Williams & Essence Best Seller Ms. Valencia Williams.

<u>Everyone at County Line Trade Center</u>

And all the readers who support me. Feel free to e-mail me at <u>sayupromise@hotmail.com</u> or better yet hook up with me at www.myspace.com/sayupromisebooks

MS. MICHEL MOORE

Who's Da Daddy?

"Damn will yall hurry the hell up and snatch this little crumb begging bastard up out of me!" Twenty-three year old unmarried and uneducated Ms. Simone Harris was lying on the cold steel delivery table with her legs cocked open wide enough for a UPS truck to drive inside. "I don't know how much more of this pain I can stand! Yank on his big head if you have to!"

Simone's all of a sudden bible toting, strict holier than thou, also unwed mother had cast a rebellious Simone out years ago leaving her to basically get that shit how she lived which was straight out scurvy. Done deal. Real talk. She had no respect for anyone not even herself.

The exhausted night nurse on duty was at the end of a long tiring shift. She was fed up, losing patience with the young girl's disrespectful demeanor. She took a cool cloth placing it on the back of Simone's neck trying to ease some of the tension in the room. "Listen here Miss. I know that it hurts to some degree, but you don't have to carry on like that." The nurse scolded. "Now try to relax and get control of yourself."

"How your old ass gonna tell me how to act?" Simone screamed out. "You ain't got no big baby dangling half out your pussy! So stop playing around and get this over! Why is it taking so long?"

Simone was out of breath from pushing. Even against the doctor's constant demands to calm down and not to force the baby out so fast, Simone was caught up with doing her own thing. In between each and every heavy pant she took, Simone found the time to curse and down rate the very nurses and doctors that were helping to bring her obviously unloved son into the world.

"Young lady, please, you have to take it easy." The doctor pleaded repeatedly. "You might injure your child."

"What about me and the way this freaking baby done injured my perfect ass!" Simone shrieked out in agony still talking cash shit. "Is anybody concerned about that?"

Thank God, two or three more pushes and several dozen insults later, Terrell Dion Harris was finally born. After the doctor went through the ritual of hitting the baby's tender behind and cutting the cord, the nurse held him up to his mother's face for her to get her first look at her son. "It's a healthy baby boy!" The doctors and nurses smiled with pride having brought another child safely into the world.

When Simone wiped the sweat from her eyes, seeing little Terrell, she went ballistic. "Bitch is you nuts or something? Why the fuck is you dripping all that mucus crap all on me?" She not once took notice of his dark wavy hair or his tiny slanted eyes that were slightly opened. There was no counting of fingers or toes, just flat out bugging. "Why don't you go do your job and clean his butt off before you bring him the hell over here? Don't nobody wanna be seeing all that slimy stuff!"

"You should be ashamed of yourself for the way you're behaving!" The nurse belted out in response. "I pity the man who fathered this innocent child. You're a disgrace to parents everywhere!"

"Just do your steppin' fetchin' job Nurse Old Ass before I crawl out this bed and smack you!" The entire delivery staff momentarily stood speechless at the young mother's rudeness. The nurse shook her head as she went about her way and cleaned the innocent newborn off.

As Simone waited to hold her baby she got increasingly angry thinking about the Ballers Shot Callers Cabaret that she would certainly miss that night. All the real true players in Detroit were gonna be flossing at that motherfucker, and here she was stuck up in a hospital room with a damn baby that she felt had stretched her womb ten sizes out of shape and caused her to gain at least thirty eight pounds.

When Simone finally held her barely minutes old son in her arms she looked at him and giggled with relief. From his light bright caramel skin to the shape of his upper lip, he was a spitting image of her and only her. Hallelujah Jesus and praise the Lord, it was not one thing about little baby Terrell that resembled his father, nan one of them. Not Joey or Kamal.

Simone kissed her son's wrinkled forehead then softly whispered in his small ear with a huge grin on her face. "Game on Lil Nigga! You about to make your Momma some real paper now! We ain't gonna want for shit!"

Chapter One

☼

"Girl, trust and believe when I tell you thangs is straight lovely for a pretty bitch like me! I just can't believe how dumb and naive these ass holes are in this freaking city. I swear to God, I have never, ever in my twenty-five years of living in the Murder Mitten, seen two bigger fools walking the face of this earth than Joey and Kamal's simple behinds. They must have been born without brains. I know that I'm the shit and all, but damn!"

Simone was sitting back, styling and profiling on her brand new plush cream leather couch, with both feet kicked up on the matching marble coffee table. She was like a Supreme Chief Justice Judge residing on the bench holding court, as she passed her own personal observations and views on different ghetto bullshit. Sporting the latest clothes, a new Lexus in the driveway, plenty of jewelry and two Negroes on her line, Simone was on top of the world and her game, so she thought.

Having given birth to a bouncing seven-pound baby boy a little over two years ago, Simone's body was finally back in tip-top perfect shape. All the weight, she'd gained during her pregnancy, managed to stay put in the right places and was toned. Ms. Thang was what many old school players referred to as *a brick house*. Simone was completely convinced, hands down, no questions asked that she was the shit and no one, man nor beast, could tell her any different. Even if they tried it wouldn't do any good, her self esteem was seriously stuck on arrogant.

"Them crazy busters ain't got a clue about nothing. They gonna both hustle to take care of me and Lil T for the next eighteen years, regardless! Flat the fuck out!"

Moving her shoulder length hair out of her face, she smirked as the tightly twisted blunt made its way around the room to her. Simone placed it up to her nose sniffing the strong funky aroma. "Hell yeah! This dat true shit!" She then put it up to her lips inhaling deeply several good times, holding the smoke in until she started to choke. Simone tried her best to gain hold of her composure taking full advantage of the blunt being in her possession.

"You watch and see." Simone hit it once again and started gagging. "The game is on!"

Her friend stared at her all of fifteen seconds, before she started to complain. "Damn, bitch! Why you gots to hog all the weed and shit?" Chari started laughing as she snatched the blunt out of Simone's hand and protested. "Other people wanna get high too. Shit!"

Chari was one of Simone's best friends in the entire world and Godmother to her son, Lil T. The two girls had been hanging out with one another ever since the fourth grade at Mc Manor Elementary, when Chari's family moved to the projects from Grove Hill, a small town located in rural Alabama, right outside of Mobile.

While Simone was high yellow in skin tone, with shoulder length golden brown hair and brown color eyes, Chari was just the opposite. The hot Alabama sun had been generous with touching her already, extra dark chocolate complexion. Chari wore short dread locked hair and her skin was overly cursed with acne, which always brought constant ridicule from the fellas as well as most of the females she would encounter. Her best friend, Simone didn't make it any better by always behaving like she was the real show-stopper.

Chari was content in playing the background position and was disgustingly loyal to Simone. She didn't mind playing the demeaning role that she was assigned in life. Chari admired her friend and loved listening to her brag about her so-called 'SKILLS'. It often passed the time away while they were getting fucked up. But the truth be told was that deep down inside, Chari really felt sorrow for her misguided friend.

Simone struggled to talk, still choking as she laughed at Chari. "Be passed careful, Girl don't be burning up my shit with them ashes." She made sure to watch her friend like a hawk. It took her two long solid months of begging and major ass kissing to get her new furniture. No matter how much crap she talked, bottom line, she knew her furniture would have to last for some time to come. It wasn't any telling when Simone's money train would pull out of the station, leaving her high and dry and flat broke looking for the next man in line to pick up the slack.

Out of the clear blue sky, Simone jumped up running over to look out the huge picture window. With the rattling noise of the metallic blinds in her ear, she carefully searched the block for any signs of movement. After peeking out, scanning the premises and not seeing jack, she went back plopping her body on the couch. The weed had taken over having Simone posted on paranoid status thinking that she was hearing things. "Dang, I swear a bitch thought I heard somebody calling my name!" Simone snickered as she finished her speech. "These trees must got me gone! Anyway Chari, now like I was saying, as long as I got Lil T, then a bitch gonna get tore off, that's a given. You feel me? In between Joey damn near furnishing this crib, and Kamal paying my car note on a monthly basis, I'm tight! Please believe!"

Simone's tiny son had taken his first steps, celebrated three birthdays and was smart for his age. But was still somewhat confused over which one of his mommy's *boyfriends,* that always took turns sleeping in her bed and lying on top of her, was his true biological father. Simone taught Lil T to call both of them Da-Da and while not fully understanding one way or the other he did as he was told. Joey and Kamal both showed Lil T unconditional love whenever they would be around and that was all that mattered to him in his little corner of the world.

   The entire nine months of Simone's pregnancy, from conception to delivery, she had both Joey and Kamal running around catering to her every whim or desire. Whether it was all expense paid shopping sprees at the local upscale mall, fresh shrimp and lobster meals or trips to the day spa to get a full body massage, including her swollen feet being rubbed, Simone had them both going in circles to please her, constantly reminding them the reason she was so fat and uncomfortable was that she was carrying their seed. Simone was out cold rolling the dice in the potentially fatal game she was playing.

   When Simone got the results from her ultrasound, she unfortunately found out it was going to be a boy she would give birth to. She had to think quickly to maintain the game that she had started. The closer her due date got the pressure was building. Joey or Kamal didn't have any children, making Simone's baby their first. She knew for a fact each of them would most certainly want his first born son, to bare his name and carry on their family legacy. In any other normal situation when a female was pregnant, married or not, naming the baby was no big deal. Yet, nothing was ever easy when it came to Simone and her fast paced confusion filled life.

After weeks of thinking and scheming, Simone devised the perfect cover to secure her future. She explained to the two devoted expectant fathers that she wanted to name the baby, Terrell Harris, after her loving father who had tragically passed away when she was just a little girl. She even managed to shed a few tears looking sincere as a fuck when she told the sad fictitious lie to each one. The crazy reality was Simone never once met her father or even knew who the buster was for that matter. She acted her ass off royally, deserving an Academy Award for Best Dramatic Performance in a Baby Daddy Lie.

Touch Down! After all the plotting that Simone went through, it paid off working like a charm. It had to. Her cash flow and everyday survival depended on it. Joey was the first one to give in to her emotional request. (Code Name for LIE) He was easy. His devotion for Simone was true. The things that he did for her and Lil T were strictly out of love. The day that Simone and the baby were due to be released from the hospital, Joey spent more than a couple of thousand on bottles, diapers and cases of formula. He purchased a brass canopy crib fit for a little Prince and enough clothes for an entire room full of babies. Joey vowed that his son would want for nothing. Simone, being the woman that carried his seed, would of course reap the benefits receiving the same treatment as their son. She was undeniably living on easy street.

Joey offered to marry Simone so they could be a real family, but she flat out refused the proposal after finding out that Joey's elderly parents would be living with them. It was no way that Joey was going to leave his folks who were both sickly and needed him the most. They'd made sure to give him the best education they could afford. Always taking him to museums, art galleries and other cultural events to ensure that he was well rounded and responsible, Joey's parents gave him everything they had.

Now was his time to repay their loyalty and the type of man he was, doing that was not a problem, but a privilege.

Kamal on the other hand was stubborn, meaning Simone had some heavy begging to do to finally change his one tracked sinister mind. He wanted the baby named Kamal Isa Jeffries Jr., after him, period point blank. He was way on the other side of the meter from Joey when it came to showing any form of compassion. If enough money was involved, he'd smack up, spit on and rob his own dying grandmother of her last grasping breath. He was spiteful, stingy and hard nosed.

Simone believed the fact that both his parents being drug addicts caused him to be so mean spirited. One late night, getting overly intoxicated, Kamal even let it slip out that him and his younger sister were both born crack babies. She was happy that she'd never met either one of his parents knowing they were the reason for most of his erratic behavior. A loose cannon from first conception Simone would always have to bring her A-Game when dealing with Kamal. The hustle was rough as hell, but the final payoff was always fucking gravy.

☼

"Girl, what you gonna tell Lil T when he gets older and shit? He's gonna want to know the truth, then what you gonna say?" Chari was honestly concerned for her God child's well being and safety as she reached on the table putting the blunt in the ashtray. She adjusted her body in the chair, relaxing as she stared at Simone, so she could hear her friend's response clearly to the question. "Then what?"

"Don't worry about all that. By the time that bullshit jumps off, please believe, I should be pushing a brand new Lexus, living in a plush lavish condo uptown and my pockets on swoll. Let me run this Chari!" Simone rolled her eyes while sucking her teeth twisting her neck. "Just get ready to ride in that new Lex, alright bitch!"

Chari hated to doubt her girl or her skills, but she knew that Simone was living foul as a motherfucker and misery was lurking around the corner waiting to pounce on her. "I ain't mad at you. Simone, I swear to God." Chari insisted raising her left hand up. "I'm just worried about Lil T and how his feelings will be hurt when this lie hits the fan." Chari's facial expression was full of doom as she frowned at the thought of the outcome. *"Everything in the dark comes to the light sooner or later."*

"Alright Ms. Worried! Stop sending all them bad vibes my way! You blowing my dang gone high. How about I see if I can get a baby sitter and we go down to the club tonight?" Simone was trying to change the subject and get Chari off her back. "You need to loosen the hell up!"

"You right Simone. I know I'm tripping." Chari tried to act as if she was done with the subject. "I'm gonna call Prayer's behind and see if that jealous negro she lives with will let her hangout."

Both girls gave each other a high five as they clowned, their friend. "Yeah, he do be acting like her damn daddy!" Simone laughed as Chari grabbed her cell phone out her purse and started to dial Prayer.

"But for real, for real. I do wish I had a man like Prayer's. He really loves her." Chari smiled.

"Whatever!" Simone replied with a sarcastic tone as she picked up the cordless phone off the charger disappearing into the kitchen. She then swung opened her well-stocked stainless steel refrigerator checking how many juice boxes Lil T had left, while calling her young neighbor, Yvette who lived just across the street with her nosey foster mother.

Any time Simone needed a baby sitter on short notice, the impressionable girl was Johnny on the spot and eager to please. Yvette looked up to her fly neighbor Simone. With all the high priced cars and trucks that frequently pulled in and out of the driveway and not to forget all the designer hand-me-downs, Simone spoiled her with, Yvette loved being at the house. Whether it was washing dishes, cleaning Lil T's toy filled room, changing his dirty pull ups or braiding his hair, the orphaned teenager would rush right over to do her undeserving hero a favor, despite her foster mother Ms. Holmes disapproving glances, who seemed to have a third eye when it came to seeing Simone for what she truly was; trouble brewing.

"Hey Simone!" Chari yelled into the kitchen. "Prayer said that ole boy is out of town, so she'll be over in about a hour or so." Chari was always happy when all three of them went clubbin'. It gave her someone to talk to when Simone would pull one of her all too famous disappearing acts and turn into a ghost. Simone was good, for meeting some wanna-be ballin' dude at the bar, getting invited to V.I.P. and leaving her friends, ass out to dry.

"Oh dig that. That's tight. Yvette's young behind is on her way over, so let me get Lil T up from his nap. Plus, I have to call Joey and see if he's going to hang out tonight or what." Simone came back into the living room starting to gather up stuff to put in an oversized Coach purse, which doubled as her son's overnight bag.

"Dang gee Simone, I thought, you, me and Prayer were just hanging tonight?" Chari questioned with a disapproving frown plastered on her face.

Simone did a double take at her girl immediately stopping dead in her tracks. Steam appeared to be rising from her head as she leered maliciously at Chari. "Listen you big crybaby. If Joey and his boys show up down at the club, we all three gonna get free drinks." Simone threw Lil T's stuff down on the coffee table out of frustration. "So unless you got some other fools to sponsor our black asses, shut the fuck up and get ya behind ready. How bout that!"

The room grew silent as Simone stormed out marching into the bedroom to get her son up and ready to go over to Yvette's. *"That bitch must be freakin nuts!"* Simone thought as she harshly shook Lil T awake from his peaceful nap. It was no way in Miami heat hell, that Ms. Simone was going to let any opportunity to eat, drink or party on someone else's fat pockets slip by. If Chari wanted to stay home and miss out on the fun, then so be it. That would be her fucking loss. Simone was about her business when it came to getting over. If it was ladies free before ten o'clock, then you better know that Simone was walking in at nine fifty nine on the nose. She was always down for whatever, especially when it wasn't costing her a damn thang!

"Hey wake up Terrell." She grabbed his little arms.

"Yes Mommy." Lil T began to cry from being instantly snatched out his teddy bear candy land dreams.

"Come on and help Mommy get your things so you can go bye-bye with Yvette."

Lil T was still half asleep as Simone stood him on his feet forcing him to walk on his own. Still considered just a baby, he wanted to fall out on the floor, whine and kick about being too sleepy to move, but was wise enough to know that his mother, Simone didn't play that shit and would smack his hand or better yet his behind.

Lil T would have been considered a blessing and Godsend to most parents, but to his mother she saw him in a much different light; a meal ticket! The two baby books Simone kept with both Joey and Kamal's names listed as the 'Daddy' was proof positive of that messy underhanded shit.

Poor misunderstood Chari, still motionless alone in the living room finally quietly sat back in the chair without muttering a single solitary word as she listened to Simone bark orders to her son. She knew, once again, that her friend was right about the night.

"I guess the fellas should come. Free is free!"

Chapter Two

☼

It was almost 8 o'clock in the evening when Prayer was pulling up in the long gravel filled driveway bouncing her man Drake's, brand new triple black Range Rover that was sitting on 22's. The sounds were on bump causing the windows in Simone's house to vibrate from the bass while all the neighborhood kids stood wide eyed and amazed at the spinners. They swarmed around to gawk, while dancing to the sounds of the music playing. It was a typical scene out of a deep down in the dirty rap video with everyone snapping their fingers, even Granny.

"Ooow weee…! That's my truck!" One kid yelled.

"No it ain't, it's mine!," screamed the next.

Chari happily ran on the porch and out to the sidewalk to greet Prayer.

"Damn chick, when did yall get this? This shit is hot to death! Yall two done moved up in the world like George and Weezy!"

"Girl, stop bugging. It ain't nothing but another bill to pay." Prayer laughed stepping out the truck, "another way for Drake's crazy ass to floss! You know how he do."

Chari completely tuned out her friend trying to down play the sweet ride she was gripping and continued to jock. No matter what Prayer said to Chari, trying to change the subject from the new truck, they both had to agree that it was the shit and Drake had truly out done himself this time.

Prayer never bragged about her house, wardrobe or money. She didn't have to. Her shit spoke for itself. This female didn't have to put on airs of superiority or degrade the next person to make her self feel better. She was living her life the way Simone dreamed about, which is probably, the reason the two hardly ever got along. Simone was secretly bitter and insecure when it came to Prayer who was equally as pretty as Simone, but carried herself with a lot more class.

"Girl, stop all that fooling and come give me a hug." Prayer opened her arms running towards Chari. They both smiled, as Chari continued praising her girl. Prayer was rocking a pair of bright white hip huggers that showed off her shape, a tight fitting tank top with flashy rhinestones across the chest that spelled out Diva, and a pair of raw gator sandals. Her toes were perfectly manicured to match her nails. She had a Christian Dior purse on her shoulder and her hair was fierce. The girl stayed on point and couldn't be faded.

"Now that's what's really up, Prayer. You keep you some fly gear on ya butt." Chari waved her hand around snapping her fingers twice as the two walked up the stairs entering Simone's front doorway.

Simone had been standing in the bedroom window watching Prayer pull up fuming with hatred from the whip Prayer was driving and the way Chari, who she thought was her private flunky, was kissing Prayer's ass. Simone wanted to see exactly what Prayer was wearing, so she could try her best to out shine her. She tore through her closet like a tornado searching for an outfit that would make both Chari and Prayer jealous. Unfortunately, the last few days that Simone tried on her clothes, nothing seemed to fit the way she liked for them to. *"Damn, I need* some new gear! Them hoes done seen most of this shit. Forget Lil T, for now on out I'm buying for self!"

Simone snatched up her phone off the bed dialing Joey's cell number. After three or four rings, he answered.

"Yeah, what's good Simone Baby?"

"What took you so long? It was about to go to voice mail." Simone rolled her eyes to the top of the ceiling as she paced the room. Her frustration in not finding an outfit was getting took out unfairly on an innocent Joey.

"Is something wrong with my Lil' Man?" He quizzed. "Is my son missing his old dude? Put him on the phone."

"Naw nigga. Don't play yourself. He ain't even here. Yvette just came and swooped his little bad butt and took him across the street. She's keeping him until I get back."

"Where is you going?" Joey instantly got pissed. "And why you calling me going off? What the fuck is your problem?"

"What, now I can't call you unless it's about my son?" Simone whined sensing Joey's anger.

"Don't you mean our fucking son?"

"Whatever Joey! You know what the hell I mean!"

Simone was now offended and started yelling at him. "Me, Chari and Prayer's stuck up ass are going out later and I ain't got shit to wear. Most of this stuff I got is way too tight." Simone quickly eyeballed her clothes. "You always talking about you love me and your son so damn much, then why a bitch ain't got no gear? Can you tell me that?"

"What did you just say?"

"You heard me Joey! I ain't gonna repeat my damn self!"

"Hold the fuck up! Is that why you blowing up my phone, cause you can't decide what to wear tonight to some club? Damn Simone, why you have to act so childish all the time? That shit ain't even cute."

"Oh and I guess I'm acting childish when a bitch be on her knee's sucking your little dick too, huh?"

"Dig that! You got jokes and shit!" Joey huffed grabbing his nuts. "Ain't shit little about this monster in my pants!"

"Naw that ain't no joke Boy. You think you just gonna keep knocking the value off my body and a bitch don't get shit out the deal except a soaking wet pussy?"

"What you mean nothing? Simone, who do you think paid for that new expensive furniture your ass over there parlaying on? The fucking couch fairy?"

Simone sighed. "Damn! Why don't you stop tripping?"

"Naw Simone, let's keep it real!" Joey insisted. "Didn't I just buy your ungrateful butt $450 worth of stuff?"

"When? What you talking about?"

"You know the fuck when! Don't play dumb. Down at *'Shhh…Our Secret Lingerie'*, ya girl Kim's spot from around the way. Don't front."

"Oh that shit don't count! Nigga you wanted to see my fine ass poured into those panties and hookups!"

"However you want to put it Simone, a guy still dropped that loot! So be easy and chill the hell out!"

Joey and his crew were posted at the park, enjoying the summer sights of females running around, half-naked. From the tiny shorts that barely covered their butt cheeks, to the thin material tops that showed their bra less breast bouncing up and down, the guys were in heaven. Most days it was like being in a strip club, without the pole or high priced watered down drinks. A brother didn't even have to come out his pockets to tip and still seen plenty of ass. At Chandler Park anything goes.

Joey was one of those rare exception to the rules type of brothers that a chick always daydreamed about, but never actually ran into. No doubt, hell yeah he'd look, the guy was human, but he never crossed the line. Joey loved spending time with both Simone and his son, Lil T, but he was growing increasingly tired of her out of the blue tantrums and outrageous demands.

Besides, his boys thought Simone was nothing more than a sack chasin' slut and often made their feelings known. Joey constantly heard the rumors circulate about Simone and her wild behavior, but still didn't care. He trusted her. She was after all, the mother of his son. Simone often pressured him for money and gifts, but enough was enough! He was starting to feel like her little Do Boy.

When Joey originally met Simone at one of the after hour spots she hung at, he was fully aware of the many challenges he would have to overcome to satisfy a woman like her. Even though he was stressed out much of the time, aggravated by Simone's sharp tongue and the barrage of insensitive words that flew out her mouth, he genuinely loved her unconditionally.

Simone was glad that the huge flat screen television in the living room was on the music channel, so her friends wouldn't be all up in her business while she was getting her beg on.

"Listen Joey, I ain't being childish and don't talk to me like that either! I don't have shit to wear." She fumed. "I bet you rockin' some fresh gear. Do you want ya baby's momma walking around the streets looking busted?" Simone was trying to sound sexy as she slowly convinced him for some money to go shopping. "Please Daddy! I love you! I love you! I love you!"

"Alright then Simone, I tell you what." Joey remorsefully replied. "Meet me down at the club later and I'll give you some loot. Now Peace!"

Joey usually made Simone sweat it out a little bit longer before he would agree, but he had to rush her off the phone. He gave in a lot quicker when he spotted a caravan of six different colored F-150's turn into the park's entrance. Simone and her bullshit had to be put on the shelf temporarily. Joey and his crew had been beefing on and off with these dudes all summer long over the Brewster Housing Projects and who could or could not sale drugs there. The uncontrolled violence was steadily increasing with each passing month. They all stayed on the six o'clock news doing ambush style slayings.

  The trucks took their time cruising the perimeter of the main strip, giving everyone, especially the females, time to jock them. Joey and his boys perched back on their rides trying to play it cool. Their hands were tightly gripped on their pistols, which were concealed by the over sized T-shirts that they wore. The hot scorching sun beamed down causing an already tense situation, to get even hotter.

  All six trucks slowly pulled onto the main strip of the park and eased in the direction of Joey and his boys. Joey could feel his heart beating extra fast the closer they got. He cautiously kept his eyes focused on each dude that occupied the passenger seats. If something was gonna jump, nine out of ten times, they'd be the shooter. The air was extremely dry and there hadn't been a breeze blow by in hours. Everything was still as if mother nature had advance warning of trouble.

"These fools act like they want some. Yall fellas be on point." Joey advised his crew and his right hand man, who stood by his side.

"I'm on it!" Trevon whispered under his breath as he waited with anticipation. "They don't want none!"

The first five trucks eased pass without incident. It was the first time that each crew really had the chance to get a good look at one another in the daylight. The driver in the last F-150, which was royal blue with gigantic tires making it sit higher than the others, took his time to mean mug, Joey's entire crew while smiling, nodding his head to the music that he was pumping. His sinister grin showed off his gold fronts. He stared extra hard and winked his eye at Joey and then BAM! Everything from that point on went in serious slow motion. Chaos and havoc checked in taking complete control over the normally quiet summer afternoon at the local park. The calm day was ruined.

"OH SHIT! WHAT THE FUCK!"

Just as the truck had almost turned the bend, two guys raised up out the flat bed and started shooting in Joey's direction. One of them was huge with long corn rolls that reached his shoulders. Him and another skinny dude had fully automatic weapons and were spraying bullets into everything that moved. Pandemonium took over the strip and the main park entrance as cars rushed out.

Joey and his boys barely had time to dive under their cars and take cover. With their faces pressed onto the germ infested pavement, each prayed not to get hit. The bullets were flying, hitting garbage cans, parked cars and empty baby strollers that mothers had abandoned. As they searched for refuge from the terror that was taking place, Joey and his crew were trapped at a disadvantage never having time to return fire.

Simone slammed the phone down. "Now that's what's up! I knew that punk ass nigga was gonna reconsider and give in. Now, I just gotta play this shit off." Focusing back at the problem at hand, she glanced in the closet finally deciding to put on a muti-colored strapless sun dress and a pair of slip on Jimmy Choo mules. The hook up wasn't new, but Simone was gonna front anyway. After putting on her make-up, she did a double check in the full length mirror admiring her self once more before making her grand entrance joining her friends in the living room.

"Hey Prayer, when did you get here? I didn't see you pull up. I was in the back talking to Joey's whining self. His crazy ass is trying to take me on a shopping spree." Simone was trying her best to sound convincing as she strolled in the room. "I told him that I was hanging out with my girls and would see him at the club later. That guy know he be sweating me!"

Simone's acting job was amusing to Chari and Prayer. They both saw the curtains in the bedroom moving before they came in and knew Simone was watching them like a hawk. Plus, Simone was not the quietest person in the world. Even with the television on, they could hear her begging Joey for money. They were her friends, so they let Simone keep her dignity and listened to her lies. They could have easily humiliated her, but Chari or Prayer weren't built like that. It was more Simone's cut throat style to kick a person while they were down.

"Hey Simone, I love this couch. This shit is butter soft. He's got good taste. Did Kamal pick this out by his self?" Prayer rubbed her hands across the leather material as she grinned changing the subject.

"Hell naw! Kamal's crazy behind ain't picked out nothing. Joey bought this for me. You know I got Kamal's behind on car note duty." Simone announced proudly poking her chest outwards. "Matter of fact, I'm thinking about upgrading from my Lexus, maybe getting a truck or something. What yall two skanks think?"

Once again Simone was fronting. Chari and Prayer looked at one another and smiled. They knew that their friend's tall tales were just beginning for the night.

"One day I'm gonna school yall two on playing these cats. God put dudes on this earth to serve females like myself. Kamal and Joey are both running around here on my chain. Me and Lil T is living hood rich!" Simone continued talking cash shit, holding court again. "It's a hard job pimping these negroes but somebody has to."

Prayer finally having enough of Simone 101 cut her off in mid speech. It was only so much she could take of Simone's annoying voice and nonsense before she needed a stiff drink.

"In my opinion…"

"Girl, it's getting late. Let's be up and out." Prayer grabbed her purse and keys, heading towards the door. "I'm ready to get my dance on!"

Chari was glad that Prayer suggested that they break camp and followed her outside leaving their girl, Simone standing in the middle of the living room by her self.

Simone being Simone had to get the last word in. "I was bout to tell yall hoes to hurry up," she informed them while grabbing her purse and locking the door before catching up.

Chari ran across the lawn and up to the Range Rover calling out shotgun like a little kid. Prayer clicked the remote, unlocked the doors and started the truck all in one movement. The music came on full blast as the girls climbed inside. Simone was trying to act all high post and didn't even acknowledge the new truck.

Although she was heated that she would have to play the back seat, she tried not to make a big deal about it. Fake ass Simone really did wanna ride in Prayer and Drake's new truck. Who wouldn't? All bullshit aside no doubt about it, the Range Rover was cold as a motherfucker, even the back seat.

Holier than thou, good hatin' ass, pissed to see the next bitch do better, Simone couldn't deny it even if she tried. But to actually speak or even let slip those simple complimentary ass kissing words out loud, from of her mouth, for the next bitch to actually hear! Especially Prayer! Oh Hell Too The Naw! Forget About It! Next!

Chapter Three

Joey and his friends slowly crawled from beneath their cars checking to make sure that no one was hit. Even though they had their hands on their pistols, not one of them expected them boys to open fire in broad daylight, in a middle of a park or be brazen enough to lie down in a back of a flat bed.

"Man them dudes is crazy! Doing that old gangsta type shit out here with all these kids running around." Joey was heated as he looked over at the swings thinking about the fact that his precious son could have been on them and killed by a stray bullet. "Them punk bitches got holes all up in my ride and look at my motherfucking windshield!" He walked around his car and couldn't believe his eyes.

"You right Joey! We gonna have to seriously deal with them cowards!" His boy Trevon screamed wiping the sweat off his forehead. "Who the fuck do they think they are, coming on our side of town with that crap?"

"Man that shit was too close. We gotta sit down and figure out a plan that's gonna make them rat ass busters catch it!" Joey started brushing the dirt off his clothes and surveying the scuffs on his new Air Force 1's. He then reached his hand inside the car putting the key in the ignition. "Let me see if this bitch gonna even crank." After three good tries the bullet riddled car shockingly started, Joey smirked. "I'm gonna bounce to the crib, switch rides, shower and change into something else. Let's meet down at Bookies later on and start plotting on them fools. After this a brother straight needs a drink. Besides, I gotta hook up with Simone anyhow."

His friends gave him a dirty foul look as soon as he mentioned Simone's name. They started to call Joey out and talk mad shit about her, but they all had a rough afternoon and were ready to get out of dodge before the police came around questioning everyone at the park.

On the way driving home, Joey couldn't help but to think about the driver of that royal blue truck and the way he looked at him. Something wasn't right with the whole way shit went down.

Joey turned his sounds down as he buried himself deep in his thoughts.

"*Damn I know that guy from somewhere other than the streets, but where? I gotta figure that shit out!*"

The line for valet was twisted clear around the corner. Bookie's was off the chain. It seemed like everyone who was anyone was trying to post up in the club. The long wait gave the trio of women time to flirt with all the guys walking by and see who was driving what. That would cut down on time inside the club, as to who was broke as shit and who was really getting that paper. Even though, Simone was pimping the back seat, she was still geeked. They were getting mad major props from all the fellas and cold blooded animosity from the envious females.

 "Damn, I have never waited this long for valet." Prayer shook her head while maintaining her place in line and a tight grip on the steering wheel. "It's obvious that it's crowded. Fuck this line!"

 "Yeah girl, it's packed in there. Do yall chicks wanna head somewhere else?" Chari added her two cent.

Simone wasn't trying to hear none of that and was the first one to respond. "Dang, it ain't that long. Yall should be happy. It's some ballers up in there. I'm bout to get my mack on, so yall hoes chill!"

Simone was on a mission to convince Prayer and Chari to be a little bit more patient and go inside. Yeah, true enough it was a few guys that went inside Bookies dressed to impress as if they were slinging that shit, so of course, that alone was reason enough for her to go in.

Yet, first and foremost Joey was gonna meet her in there and it was no way in hell, Simone was gonna miss out on getting the loot he'd promised her earlier. Simone was going inside the club and wait it out for her money even if it meant she had to jump out of the moving truck and go in that bitch solo.

After a few more minutes passed, the girls made it up to the front of the line. Prayer had a bootleg mix C.D. blasting, as they rocked their heads from side to side. All eyes were, without a doubt, on them. Simone was basking in all the status they were getting from pulling up in a pimped out new ride. Prayer pumped the brakes repeatedly causing the Range Rover to dance before they screeched to a halt. Part two of the Dirty South video was happening as everyone leaned with it, to the sounds.

The guys working valet, as well as the people standing out front, were staring and smiling as the trio of ghetto diva superstars made their exit from the truck. Simone and Chari both stood beside the truck holding shit down in the spotlight while waiting for Prayer to give the Valet her keys.

"Here you go." Prayer slid him ten extra dollars to park her shit up front. "Put my truck at the doorway Sweetie!"

"Not a problem! Yall ladies have a nice evening." The Valet couldn't wipe the silly grin off his face as he watched the three walk away.

Chari, Simone and Prayer marched to the front of the line with confidence. No sooner than the bouncer saw them approaching, he pushed opened the door. They were all regulars at the club. The manager of Bookies knew that every time Simone was in the house, guys would buy her and her girls top shelf drinks. He anxiously anticipated making a lot of money from the bar.

She was good for business. Simone might have been reckless when it came to treating her friends with respect, but flat out, she was a true hustler. No one could knock her ability to play the game. When she put her mind to getting something, she usually achieved her goal. Simone was so good at talking junk, dudes would be popping bottles until their money ran low and then she'd often times abandon them where they stood, moving on to the next fool in a matter of minutes.

   The club was almost packed to capacity and the crowd was hyped. Simone took the lead as they cut across the dance floor making their way to the bar. Until Joey got there, she had to find another sucker to buy her a drink.

"Come on. Let's go on the other side of the room." Simone was smooth flowing in and out of the sea of people. "Hey, it looks like those guys who were bouncing that red BMW that were in front of us are standing over in the corner. I'm gonna see if I can get on!"

"Dang, why don't you slow down?" Chari asked.

"Just hurry up before some other hoe beats me to the punch!" Simone frowned back at her friends.

Prayer was also trying to keep up with Simone, and finally gave up. "Chari, forget chasing her ass to try to get a free drink from some losers. I ain't got time for that, I got us."

"Good looking out Prayer you can just order me an apple martini, with two olives."

"That's sounds good as hell. I'm gonna get me one too." Prayer squeezed her small frame body up to the bar to order both their drinks as she watched Simone push up on the guys trying to work her magic.

Chari saw some people leaving one of the booths and quickly grabbed the table. She took a piece of tissue out of her purse and wiped it off. Just as Chari finished and was sitting down, Prayer was bringing over the drinks.

"They're busy as hell at the bar. I just took a napkin full of olives my damn self." She sat down and took a small sip handing the other glass to Chari. "Damn, this is good. How's yours?"

Chari was preoccupied with staring at a dude that was sitting back at a table across the room. She knew he was out of her league, but that didn't stop her from checking him out. He was more Simone's type. Even though he was flirting back, Chari was so brainwashed by her girl she wasn't even sure what day it was most of the time when it came to men or relationships. Simone, always had a bad habit stepping in, coming between any guy that showed an interest in Chari, whether she truly wanted him or not.

Prayer nudged her friends' arm to bring her out of the trance she was in. "Earth to Chari, calling Earth to Chari. Come in. Do you hear me? I repeat. Do you hear me?"

"I'm sorry Girl. I was paying attention to something else." Chari laughed as she nodded her head towards the guy.

"I feel you. He is a cutie." Prayer agreed.

The two of them sat back enjoying the music, the atmosphere and their drinks. Even though it was loud and crowded, they needed the time alone to recover from all of Simone's antics and insults.

"That chick is out of her rabbit ass mind. How long does she think it's gonna take before that baby daddy shit hits the fan?" Prayer took another sip of her drink nodding her head in agreement with Chari. "You ain't never lied.

Everything in the dark always comes to light. Karma will come around one fucking day, sneak up, and bite that ass every single time!"

"I'm just scared for Lil T because he's so innocent and didn't ask for or deserve any of this mess." Chari added. "I just know when the shit does hit the fan, he's the one that's gonna suffer." Prayer regretfully shrugged her shoulders as she took another sip. "Simone's ass don't care. Dumb bitch!"

   Both of the girl's calm and peaceful time came to an unfortunate halt when Simone found her way to the table. Her big BMW mission must have failed, because she was only holding a small glass of cheap wine, but she did have Joey and his boys in tow behind her, so her begging must have been cut short.

"I was wondering where yall broke hoes was at?"

   Simone was trying to be funny and show off in front of the fellas. Neither Chari nor Prayer laughed at their so-called friend, and her harsh comments. The true fact of the matter was Prayer held a Masters Degree in Business Management pulling in a nice fat paycheck every week and Chari was a full time student who still managed to fit in a forty hour week working at the local mall.

Both girls had more money saved in their own personal bank accounts, than the one tracked mine, unemployed Simone begged from both of her baby daddy's combined. Still, she was their girl, so they put up with her. But you know what they say. It's only so much a person can take, then just like that, you snap! If they lived in the animal kingdom Simone's half cooked ass would've been torn apart and spit out in no time flat.

"We can all squeeze in here. Yall slide over." Simone pushed Prayer's arm, whom along with Chari, obliged making room in the booth. They liked Joey much more than they liked Kamal. Joey seemed to genuinely care about Simone and Lil T. Yeah, Joey did his dirt, like all men do, but he never tried to disrespect Simone in her face.

Now Kamal was truly a horse of a different color. Any time he and Simone would get into it and she got to running off at the mouth, he would kick her ass right on the spot and take back most of the shit he bought her. Her car would stay on Repo from his ass. He didn't care if they were out in public, in the middle of a busy street or in the crib chillin' alone on a Saturday night. It made him little or none. Kamal would drag Simone's name through the mud on a regular with his family and friends. The fact that she was his son's mother meant absolutely nothing to Kamal if he was pissed off. Rest assured, he was the number one poster child for Wife Beater of the Year. He was legendary around Detroit for whopping a bitch ass at a drop of a dirty dime.

"What you ladies drinking this evening?" Joey was being big spender and treating, just like Simone anticipated.

"Apple Martinis, with extra olives." Chari spoke up.

"Thanks Joey." Prayer winked her eye.

Simone didn't want to be left out or out done with the gratitude, so she kissed Joey on his lips to show him her appreciation. *"Let's see these hoes top this!"* She thought to her self, as she gave her girls a fake smile.

Joey waved his hand at the waitress several times before finally catching her attention. When she finally fought through the thirsty crowd making it over to take their order, Simone tried to check her.

"Damn, is it that busy, that you keep top paying customers waiting all night?" Simone made sure to talk extra loud, so everyone could hear her blatant attempt to humiliate the young girl. "You must be new!"

Joey, Prayer and Chari looked at Simone like she was crazy with three heads growing out of her neck. She still had a half of a drink left in her hand that she claimed the fool pushing the BMW bought her when she first came in, so it was no legitimate reason for her to trip or make a scene.

Trevon and the rest of the fellas shook their heads at Joey and laughed. He knew exactly what they were thinking and that they were 100% right. Simone had no class whatsoever. It was as if she was raised with no home training to say the least. Joey didn't want to seem soft, besides Simone was out of order and needed a reality check in the worst type of way.

"Simone, why you gotta act such a God damn fool all the time? What the fuck is the matter with you? Are you high or something?" Joey was pissed off and read her the riot act. "We came here to relax and have a good time and shit. Why you gotta try to ruin it? We almost got killed this afternoon and your ass worried about waiting ten minutes for a free drink. That's real fucked up!" Joey gave her a long cold stare taking a deep breath. "Damn!"

Joey turned to the waitress that was still standing there overjoyed that he'd taken up for her, and tore off two crisp hundred-dollar bills lightly closing it up in her hand.

"Here you go Sweetheart, I'm sorry for all the confusion. Now what's your name?"

"It's Tami," she blushed gleefully as she took the money. "Well Ms. Tami, with your cute self, let me get three apple Martinis and double shots of Remy for all the fellas." Joey rubbed her hand. "You can keep the change."

"Thank you! I'm very sorry it took me a while to get over here to you." Her eyes were glued on Joey. "Tonight is kinda packed and…"

Before the young girl could take a cop, she was stopped.

"Naw Tami Baby, thank you!" He cut her off. "I know it's busy." Joey went out of his way to be extra nice and flirt with the waitress. He knew good and damn well that Simone would be pissed off to the tenth degree. Tami was happy as she bolted to place their orders making sure to put a little extra shake in her ass knowing that Joey was watching. The change from their bill would probably be her biggest tip all night.

Simone was fuming by this time. In a matter of moments Joey had managed to flip the script on her. She was passed being embarrassed, not only in front of Joey's boys, who she knew despised her, but worst of all Chari and Prayer, the two that she always tried to front on. It was nothing left for her to do, but sit there stick her lips out and pout like a small child.

As bad as Simone wanted to spit directly in his face and storm out, she couldn't. Joey hadn't given her that dough he'd promised her yet, so she had no choice but to chill. Heated as Simone was about getting disrespected right in her face, obtaining that cash revenue, was still first on the agenda, so she tried to sit back and relax.

In no time flat, the waitress, Tami quickly came back with the drinks on a tray and sat them down on the table, making sure to rub her breast on Joey's arm while bending over.

Once again Simone sucked it up, but not before throwing shade on the over friendly sassy female.

Everyone saw the fury on Simone's face as they grabbed their glasses and started to get their buzz on. Each person at the table was happy that she was finally getting a tiny dose of her own medicine. The night had just gotten started and Simone had already accumulated strike one in Joey's book.

Prayer heard what Joey said about almost getting killed and was concerned. Her man Drake was also deep off into the game, but on a much higher level than hand to hand street sales, thank God, but the risk and odds of getting knocked or murdered were just as high, if not higher.

"What do you mean killed?" She hated the violence that always came along with selling drugs, but that's the life that all three Joey, Kamal and even Drake had chosen. That fast money was why Simone was attracted to both of her *son's fathers*. Their personal safety came second to her finances.

Prayer's relationship was built on pure love. She met Drake back in kindergarten, before crack was born.

"Thanks for asking Prayer. I'm glad someone around here cares about if a person lives or dies." Joey made sure to look an already aggravated, Simone extra hard in her face. "It ain't nothing Prayer. Some Cats from the other side of town, fell through the park today and called they selves lighting that bitch up."

Trevon threw his hands up and grinned looking at Joey. "All that shooting and the only thing they killed, was a few cars."

"Don't remind me!" Joey fumed.

Everyone at the table busted out laughing, except a stoned faced Simone. Her cell phone started to ring and she quickly glanced down at the screen seeing that it was Kamal. "Ah fuck!" Simone mumbled under her breath as her heart started to skip a beat. It was no way she could answer the phone in Joey's face. Plus Kamal would hear the music blasting in the back round and bug out because she was at the club hanging without his permission. That type of trouble she didn't need or want so she decidedly ignored his call.

"Let Kamal's lunatic hot headed ass leave a freaking message." Simone thought as she sat next to Joey, still agitated by his straight forward act of putting her in her place. Five minutes later the phone rang again, but this time Simone didn't even bother to look at the screen she just disregarded it all together. *"Things are already going bad enough this night. I ain't hardly in the mood for his crap too!"*

Simone sat straight up in her seat tapping her fingernails on the table, waiting it out until she could find the perfect opportunity to get her cash that was promised.

Chapter Four

"Damn Kamal! That shit at the park was off the chain!" Big Ace smiled as he rolled a blunt thinking about the earlier violence.

"Yeah, you right! Did you see them little bitch ass fools crawling under they rides like scared little girls?" Kamal was enjoying all the turmoil that he believed him and his crew had caused at the park.

"I'm bout to turn on the television to see if that shit made the ten o'clock news." Big Ace announced excitedly as he clicked the remote. "I know it had to."

Kamal agreed with his boy and leaned back on the dingy plaid couch to see just who had suffered injuries from their rampage and assault. He opened a beer and lit a cigarette as he thought about the dude at the park earlier that called him self mean mugging him. The smoke from the Newport filled the air as Kamal squinted.

"That nigga acted like he knew me and shit. Like the shit was personal and not fucking business. Where do I know that lil faggot from?"

After waiting fifteen minutes for the news to come on they continued to watch the broadcast intensely for any mention, but were disappointed.

"I can't believe that shit didn't make the news!" Big Ace coughed as he passed the blunt to Kamal. "I know for a fact that I hit one of them motherfuckers!"

"Fuck it Dogg! It ain't nothing." Kamal inhaled a few good times before passing it back to his boy. "When we really break they asses off, that shit ain't gonna be local, that shit gonna be on CNN breaking news!"

"I'm tired of waiting! Them niggas should have known better than to try to set up camp in our territory!" Big Ace slammed his fist in the wall causing the huge loose paint chips to fall to the floor. "They got the game all fucked up! Them projects is ours! Nan one of them ain't get our approval to slang in that spot!"

"Oh please believe the hype. The clock is ticking on them hoes." Kamal grabbed his beer off the table guzzling the rest of it down. "Damn! Speaking of hoes, let me call my baby momma and see where the hell she at, a nigga like me want some pussy."

Kamal rubbed his semi-hard dick with one hand as he dialed Simone's number. After the fourth ring, it was apparent that she wasn't answering. On the fifth ring her voice mail clicked on and an enraged Kamal went straight Postal on her using the harshest words he knew in his small vocabulary.

"Listen up you rotten mouth bitch! I know you see my damn number! You best to stop playing games with a pimp and call me the fuck back or when I see you, I'm straight busting that ass!" Kamal was holding the phone in his face, tilting his head from side to side as he yelled into it. "Where the hell you got my son at this late anyway tramp? Call me!"

Kamal flipped his cell phone closed tossing it on the floor causing the clip on the back to break in two. He then took his size 12 Tims kicking over the two blue milk cartons that served as a makeshift coffee table. Kamal shook his head glancing slightly over at his boy with a facial expression of disgust. He had just about enough of Simone and her slut like ways. It was starting to take a serious toll on him. Although he tried to fuck everything that hopped, jumped or skipped, he wanted her to be his and only his. Even when he would disappear, spending days and nights ripping and running the streets, he was hard on his girl.

"You know what Big Ace? Simone is begging for me to stump a mud hole in that ass! She be on some other type of bullshit!" He complained rubbing the two-inch long scar on the side of his face.

Big Ace was sick and tired of Kamal always going off on Simone, day after day. To him it was nothing more than a waste of time. He knew Simone from way back when growing up in the projects and always hated her and her arrogant ways. They weren't enemies growing up, but they sure weren't friends either. Nowadays Simone acted like her family never had roaches, sharing their meatless dinners and their utilities shut off on the regular.

"For real though, Kamal man, no disrespect to ya son, you know a brother gots mad love for Lil T, but forget

Simone! You can't patrol that trick! That shit is in her blood! Her Moms was an old school whore."

Big Ace was with Kamal the night that he'd first met Simone or rather won her in a crap game. The low life guys' arm who she was proudly hanging on was over five thousand in the hole. That's when Mr. Smart Ass came up with the bright idea, to put his woman Simone up for collateral. The out of luck gambler saw the way Kamal and every other negro in the spot was checking her out and decided to take a chance.

Three rolls of the dice later, Simone was standing on the other side of the room, property of Kamal. The fact that she would jump ship that easy or not even put up a fight about being disrespected like that by her Man should've been a red flag to Kamal. But it was the complete opposite as he began parading his prize Simone around town even making her Wifey.
Big Ace tried to warn his boy about Simone from jump, but Kamal wouldn't listen. He had to have her. Big Ace and her had a strange back in the day history so he knew.
"Man, calm down." Big Ace wisely suggested.

"Dude I'm telling you I be wanna to kill that bitch!" Kamal looked up to the ceiling. "I ain't bullshitting!"

"Dig this here. Let's go down to the club and find some real little freaks to get fucked up with." Big Ace tried his best to diffuse his boy's anger. As he awaited Kamal's response he leaped to his feet and started to dance. "Well, what about it my Nigga? How you gonna carry it? You with me or not Playboy?"

Kamal gave his boy some love and nodded. "You right dude. Fuck that slutbag! Let's get clean and be out! I'll deal with Simone's slimy ass later."

After polishing off a second round of martinis, Simone, Chari and Prayer started drinking shots with the fellas. "Can you ladies handle drinking with the Big Dogs?" Joey was fucked up slurring his words as he raised his glass in the air. "This that shit ya rookies don't know jack about. That Hen Doggy Dog!" The entire table was high out their minds. All the guys were taking their shots like troopers, barking each time their glasses slammed down on the tabletop, while the ladies tried unsuccessfully to hang.

Simone had no choice, after downing the third round. She was buzzing like everyone else and back to her normal annoying self. With her dress hiked up pass her upper thigh, she was all over Joey. Covering his face with kisses and rubbing her curvaceous body seductively on his, she wanted to make it perfectly clear to the waitress, Tami and every other chick in the place that Joey was her meal ticket. So point blank, hands the fuck off! Anyone that crossed that line tonight would feel Simone's wrath.

The D.J. had the crowd jumping and the dance floor packed. He was playing everything from rap and reggae to every slow song you or your momma could think of. "Hey does anyone want to dance?" Chari was snapping her fingers, feeling good and lifted. She was ready to get her grind on and didn't care with who. "Come on Trevon! Get ya' fine ass up and let's do the damn thang!"

Trevon was on front street, blushing as he took her up on her offer or rather, demand. He stood up, while reaching for Chari's hand, who was busy trying to squeeze pass her girl. Simone was resting her head on Joey's shoulder and sticking her tongue in his ear.

"Dang, excuse me! Can a bitch get pass you two love birds?" Chari giggled as she made her way to the dance floor with Trevon close behind, being a typical man watching her ass jiggle as she walked.

Simone was getting horny as hell and started rubbing on Joey's throbbing manhood. She was slowly moving her hips to the sound of the music.

"Girl you better stop playing with a grown ass man! Do you know what you doing?" His dick was jumping from the pressure of Simone's hand. "You gonna mess around and wake this monster all the way up!"

"Yeah, I'm holding on to what's mine. That's what I'm doing. Is it a problem Joey?" Simone licked her lips slowly as she tightened her grip. "And let him wake up! I got something for his ass!"

Joey put his hand on top of hers and moved his shit to the other side of his pants. "Do you want something else to drink Baby?" He affectionately asked. Joey was high forgetting all about the incident that happened earlier. His hookup was now hard as a brick and Simone was wide open, acting as if anything goes. Joey wanted her good and faded so he could get some later without hearing her moan and groan about money.

   Simone reached across the table grabbing Prayer's glass putting it up to her mouth. "Girl let me have the rest of this until the waitress gets her slow ugly self over here."

   Prayer didn't have a chance to answer one way or another. Simone was already turning the glass up and slamming it down on the table. Prayer leaned over putting her arm around Simone. "Listen girl, you better slow the hell down and behave. Ya behind is way too twisted."

"What ever Bitch! Stay out my business! My man bought the drink for ya ass anyhow!" Simone dismissed Prayer's legitimate concern trying to be a friend.

"Oh it's like that? You think I couldn't have afforded a five dollar drink?" Prayer laughed out loud as she waved her diamond engagement ring in Simone's face. "I'm gonna give you a pass on that one Sweetie cause now I see you're more fucked up than I thought."

"Yeah Prayer, do you and let me do me!"

"Alright then Playgirl, roll with it!"

"Good! Then that's what's up!" Simone hissed.

Prayer was wise and had stopped doing shots two rounds ago. She knew her limitations when it came to drinking. Besides, she had to drive home, and it was no way, that she could even get a scratch on her man's new truck. Especially hanging out with Simone's good for nothing trifling behind.

Drake, just like all of Joey's crew, hated her. Prayer was glad he was occupied down in B-More on business, so she wouldn't have to get cursed out for spending time with her supposed to be friend and caught up in her madness. It was no two ways about it. Simone's name was mud all over town. East to West! North to South! Coast to motherfucking coast!

The music slowed down to a more relaxed pace as a heavy panting Chari finally showed back up to the table. She face was sweating buckets of perspiration and her clothes were drenched. "Damn, it was hot out there! I need some H2O." She was fanning herself with her hand trying to catch her breath. "I'm getting to old to be dancing all hard like that!"

Joey started smiling while passing her a napkin. "It looks like you went swimming and shit. Where's my boy? Did you leave his ass backstroking in the river?"

Prayer, Simone and Joey joined together in laughing relentlessly at an angry Chari.

"Forget yall! I'm here to party! Not sit around trying to look all cute! Yall some haters!" Chari barked at them.

"Come on girl, don't trip! We were just playing. Now come on, let's go to the bathroom and see if we can try to get your shit back together!" Prayer got up pulling an agitated Chari by the arm. "But for real doe, you look a hot mess!" Prayer was still laughing as Chari continued wiping away the sweat as they merged in with the crowd and found their way to the crowded ladies room.

With her girls out of the way, a drunken Simone started in on Joey. It didn't matter, how many drinks she would have in her, when it came to getting her money, Simone always sobered up quick. "When you gonna give me my dough?" she whined as she tried her best to manipulate Joey who was watching her lips move and had one thing in mind. "You promised!"

Simone took a sip of his drink and leaned back in the booth not bothering to cover her mouth when she belched. Joey over looked Simone's obnoxious behavior and kept his mind on the bigger picture.

"I got you, don't worry. I got everything you need and more." Joey was planning on getting some of Simone's famous head before the night ended.

His dick was getting harder and harder. Simone, on the other hand, was starting to feel dizzy.

"Baby, I feel sick. I think I'm gonna throw up," she warned as she put her hand over her mouth slightly gagging.

Joey jumped up without a second thought. "Well don't do that shit on me! Why didn't you take ya drunk ass to the bathroom with ya girls?" He was getting fed up with her.

"I'm sorry Baby. Can you please help me to the bathroom? I don't think I can make it."

"Damn, come the fuck on!" Joey snatched her up. "Why you always gotta be on that over the top filled crap constantly? Your ass should know better than to mix dark and light liquor."

As he complained loudly the waitress, Tami emerged from the crowd approaching the table.

"Is everything all right?" Tami placed her hand on Joey's shoulder and winked her eye. "Can I do something to help?"

Before Joey could part his lips to respond, a tipsy Simone answered for him. "Listen chick. We good alright! Now for the record, this is my fuckin' man you skank two-dollar tip gettin' hoe! And we don't need shit from ya' ass, but to keep running them drinks! Now scram! And stop slow stalking what's mine! Is we clear or what?"

Joey was tired of hearing Simone talk shit and roughly yanked her arm, dragging her towards the bathroom. "You better keep it moving!" She hissed back at the waitress as she held onto Joey's arm. "I mean it!"

"Come your silly ass on Simone, before you fall the hell out on this floor!" Joey tried his best to navigate through the sea of people that were packed into Bookies getting their groove on.

"I'm trying to keep up Joey!"

"Well try harder."

"Stop bossing me around."

"Girl, shut up and come on! I ain't got time for this!"

"What you got time for, that ugly little buck tooth waitress that insists on riding ya dick?"

"Just come on!"

    Joey felt relief when he saw the Men's bathroom finally in sight. He was glad she had to throw up because that would mean five minutes of peaceful silence from the nagging sounds of hearing Simone run her big ass boisterous mouth.

Chapter Five

☼

"Damn Cuz! This joint is packed!" Kamal looked down at his clothes and knew that he was tight. He grinned as he checked his gold fronts out in the truck mirror "I'm gonna find me a hot one tonight, for sure!" Paying careful attention to his surroundings, Kamal then checked out all the cars and other trucks. "Damn that black Range Rover parked up front is cold! I wonder who's bouncin' that motherfucker? I should check them rims in tonight."

"Dude, I feel you. It is a beast! But on another note, ain't nothing in that spot, but wall to wall girls, waiting for daddy!" Big Ace smoothed his corn rolls out. "I'm gonna be on it!'

Kamal pulled his F-150 up on the curb across the street from the club taking up two parking spaces. He was beefing with so many different cliques, getting blocked in wasn't an option. Just as they'd finished parking and were downing a fifth of Gin, finishing off a blunt, two girls strolled pass the truck on the way to the club and made sure to put extra pep in their step hoping to entice the unknown occupants of the truck.

"Hey Baby! Bring that phat ass over here!" Kamal was loud and rude as he dangled his body out the window. "Let me get ya number so I can hit them guts later!" He blurted out having the manners of a hog.

The females who were disgusted turned back getting a good look at exactly who the driver was. After seeing Kamal's wicked face, the two immediately sped their pace up in entering the club doors.

"Ain't that those dudes from the park?" One girl asked the other, as they paid the cover charge.

"Yeah, that's they crazy asses. That fool Kamal ain't no joke." She shook her head thinking about the harm he could have caused from that park stunt. "He needs to be locked under the jail for that dumb shit him and his reckless crew pulled earlier. Instead, he chilling outside showboating in his truck like he ain't did shit! That dude is pure evil!"

"Girl, I just hope he don't start no mess in here!"

"You ain't never lied!"

The guys watched them disappear behind the doors and laughed as they continued to drink and pop ecstasy pills. "Man fuck those freaks! Let's down the rest of this and go in there and find some real women." Big Ace reasoned with Kamal, his partner in crime.

After fighting a long line to get into the bathroom, Chari and Prayer took care of their business and were almost back at the table. Before they could maneuver their bodies through the crowd, something caught their attention. They stopped to listen to some girls, who had just come in, talking about a dude name Kamal, who had shot up the park earlier that day. Prayer and Chari stood in shock and disbelief, not fully comprehending what they'd just overheard.

"I hope that it wasn't Simone's Kamal they're talking about." Chari whispered to Prayer holding her arm tightly.

"Girl! You and me both!"

After continuing to listen, they found out that the dude drove a royal blue F-150 and had gold fronts. That's when they knew for a fact, that it was indeed Kamal. But the most important thing that Chari and Prayer overheard the two females say was that Kamal and his boy were parked right outside the club and would probably be coming in at any given moment.

"Oh my God! We gotta tell Simone this!" Chari ran across the dance floor towards the table, rudely bumping into people without offering one 'excuse me' or 'pardon me' on the way.

Prayer was trailing behind Chari, right on her heels displaying the same disregard for others. "Hurry up girl!" Prayer's heart was pounding from fear. She was scared for Simone, herself and everyone else in the club that would be caught in the middle of the pandemonium and turmoil if Kamal and Joey's paths crossed and they were forced to lock horns.

They were almost back at the table when the two came close to knocking down a chick that was dressed like a low income whore on the prowl. The female and her girls acted like they wanted drama and if it would've been any other time, Prayer and Chari would've stepped up and granted the bitches their wish, but they were busy trying to save Simone's ass so they gave them a pass.

When they got to the table they saw no Joey and no Simone. What they did find was Joey's boys ordering two bottles of Moet, kicking back.

"Hey Trevon, where is Simone at?" Chari nervously questioned as she scanned the room.

"Simone who?" They laughed. "We don't know anybody named Simone."

Prayer was getting heated pushing Trevon's shoulder hard. "Man, why don't yall stop playing. For real, this is serious. Where are Simone and Joey at?"

The guys were rolling over laughing by this point holding their stomachs. "Damn Prayer, you trying to go all hard now? Don't front, you know you hate that sack chaser as much as we do! That back-stabber ain't hardly yall friend!"

Chari and Prayer listened to the words coming out of Trevon's mouth and knew that a small portion of them would gain no better pleasure than seeing Simone suffer getting what she finally deserved. As much as they would like to stand idly by and watch the fireworks that were sure to take place if Kamal and Joey bumped heads, they stood by their girl. "Come on yall! Stop playing!" Chari pleaded with tears in her eyes. "Where are they at?"

"Joey took her drunk dirt ball ass to the bathroom." Trevon finally decided to stop clowning long enough to say. "About ten minutes ago."

"We just came from that way and we didn't see her." Chari yelled. "I need to talk to her it's important!" They had to put Simone up on what they'd just overheard and find a way to get her out of the club.

"I just told you where the tramp went. So go look in there for the bitch and stop acting all Federal questioning my black ass!" Trevon shouted.

"The line for the ladies bathroom is too long." Joey hesitated for a second. "You gotta go in the Men's. Ain't nobody in there, come on!"

"Joey, I can't go in there." Simone slurred.

"What ya' ass gonna do, throw up on the dance floor?"

"Naw but…"

"But what?" Joey was getting frustrated.

"Okay, but stay in there with me!" Simone's face was fire engine red.

"I ain't gonna leave ya drunk ass open like that. How you gonna play me?"

Joey put his arms around his son's mother helping her into the Men's bathroom and finding an empty stall. Simone saw the toilet and as almost on cue she started to spit up all the liquor that was in her system and what was left of her lunch and dinner. Joey was disgusted by the smell, but continued to hold her hair out of her face. He firmly gripped it in a ponytail rubbing her neck as she worshipped the white porcelain God.

"Thank you Sweetheart." Simone smiled as Joey helped her off of the filthy floor.

"I swear I be trying to have you and Lil T's back." He looked into her eyes. "Why you have to trip on a brother all the time? I let ya' ungrateful butt stay up in my pockets. What else you want, huh?"

"I don't know." Simone shrugged her shoulders regretful for some of her disrespectful actions as she turned the water on in the sink leaning over to rinse her mouth out from the foul taste of vomit.

  Joey was instantly mesmerized by Simone's ass bending over and felt his manhood rise again. He wrapped his arms tightly around her waist and slowly started grinding his dick against her. She closed her eyes and didn't protest his actions. Simone turned to face Joey grinning as she grabbed his hand leading him back in the stall shutting the door behind them. She unfastened his pants massaging Joey's throbbing dick with one of her still wet hands while pulling her dress up with the other.

  "Come get it Daddy." Simone teased eagerly. "I've been a bad girl, so punish me!"

  Joey wasted no time quickly bending Simone over, snatching her thong to the side and ramming all nine inches inside of her warm moist inners as she squirmed with enjoyment.

"Damn! Damn! Fuck me harder!" She begged and pleaded as if they weren't in a public place.

  Joey didn't show Simone any mercy as he reached down grabbing a hold of her hair once more, making her scream out his name in pain and sensual passion repeatedly as her body jerked from the force.

After ten minutes of a constant assault on Simone's sore pussy, Joey moaned and busted a nut removing his still harden dick. He wiped the head off with tissue and zipped his pants up. "I'm gonna get some more of this when we get back to your crib." He spanked her on the ass.

Simone was shook up from all the pounding and leaned forward throwing up again. Her once flawless make up and perfect hair was out of order and in serious need of attention that only a female could render.

"I'm bout to go get your friends so they can take you in the ladies bathroom and try to help you." Joey kissed her gently on her forehead and left. "I'll be right back!"

Simone knew she was sick and surprisingly didn't argue. She sat down on the toilet and waited patiently for Joey to return with Chari and Prayer. Several guys came in to take a piss and Simone didn't flinch or blink an eye. She was excessively fucked up at that point to care even if Michael, Freddy or Jason came in the place. One of them would have to kill and drag her body out for her to move.

"Alright player, let's break out." Kamal turned off the ignition and clicked the locks on the F-150.

"I'm right behind you my Dude." Big Ace climbed his 240- pound frame out the truck and brushed the ashes from the blunt off his pants. "Time to get on."

"Well then, let's get to it!" Kamal threw his hands in the air as they approached Bookies front door. There was no line outside and security must've been on break.

An older guy and a woman were coming out and accidentally bumped into an already high Kamal.

"Guy is you insane or what? You betta watch ya' step!"

"Sorry friend. My mistake, I didn't see you." The man was overly apologetic not wanting any trouble.

Kamal didn't give a shit about the man's remorse. He had to show his ass in front of a female, no matter what age, and hauled off sucker punching the man dead in his jaw, causing blood to squirt out and him falling backwards into his woman's arms resulting in the pair hitting the pavement. The woman started to yell for the absent security, but was quickly silenced by Kamal.

"I'm not your damn friend Playboy. The next time you come out of a door, pay the fuck attention where you going. Ya' follow?" He demanded pointing downwards as he towered over the injured man.

Big Ace and Kamal, showing no sympathy for the couple, went inside the club as they laughed hysterically at the man and his woman who were both left stunned and shocked at what had just taken place.

Once inside the packed walls, they were both patted down and searched for any weapons. The D.J. was playing a new song from an up and coming rap artist named Young Foy and the dance floor was packed. The club was dimly lit across the rest of the interior, but the entrance where Kamal and Big Ace stood was well lighted. The two friends took a minute trying to adjust their eyes to the sudden change from outside.

Chari and Prayer bent the corner running smack into Joey. "Oh snap, I was just coming back to the table to get one of yall to help a brother out!"

"Hey Joey! Where's Simone?"

"Yeah, we were just looking for you and Simone." Prayer stated trying not to look suspicious as she glanced over Joey's shoulder nervously.

"Well you found me," he smirked, "but ya girl is in need of some serious assistance."

"What's wrong?" A puzzled Chari asked eye balling the entrance. "Where is she?"

"She's drunk and out her rabbit. The Women's bathroom was too crowded, so I had to take her to the Men's." Joey's dick started to tingle thinking about finishing up what him and Simone started in the bathroom.

"Oh… that's why we didn't see her pass us." Prayer was without a doubt, relieved that Simone hadn't stepped out front to get some air and ran into Kamal's crazy self.

Joey shook off his short lived daydream. "I left her sloppy ass in there, calling Earl, until I could locate one of you two to play nurse mate."

"Okay, thanks Joey. We can handle it from here. We'll get Simone together and meet you back at the table." Chari forced a half a smile.

Joey didn't respond to Chari's words as a stern and treacherous expression suddenly graced his face. He was busy focusing on the front door. Chari's eyes darted back in the direction of the door and her heart fell to her feet. Kamal and his boy had just come in and were getting searched. Prayer turned pale and her mouth got dry, wishing that she would have listened to her man, Drake and not even hung out with Simone's bad luck ass.

Joey's normal ordinary happy go lucky demeanor was quickly turning before the girls' eyes. "I know that ain't that buster?" Joey mumbled under his breath. His total attention was engulfed by Kamal's every movement. If Kamal blinked twice or even farted, Joey would've seen the air blow out his ass. He was on the guy! Real talk!

Chari was panic stricken leaving Prayer and Joey standing there to make small talk. Without wasting anymore time she rushed into the bathroom. "Simone! Simone!" She yelled in a frenzy like manner, as if the club itself was on fire. The few guys that were standing up taking a leak never missed a beat, because females were out cold these days and would say or do just about anything. Chari bursting in the Men's John was just another part of a typical wild night at the club. They laughed as they left out the bathroom.

"Where the hell are you at?" Chari yelled loudly. After looking on the floor and seeing her girl's sandals, she pushed open the stall door and snatched a worn out Simone to her feet. "We gotta get the fuck out of here!"

"I know Chari. I'm sick I think I drank too much."

"Hold tight! Forget what you had to drink. You gonna be sick for real if you don't get your ass out this bathroom and out of this club!" Chari insisted.

"Girl, slow ya' roll. Just let me sit back down for a few more minutes."

Simone stumbled backwards trying to reason with her frantic friend who was scared to death.

"Listen good Simone! Pay attention! I ain't playing around!" Chari grabbed her girl's face looking her dead in her bloodshot eyes and delivered the harsh news. "Kamal and Big Ace just came in the club! They're here!"

"WHAT!" Simone sobered up on the spot. "What the fuck did you just say?"

"You heard me! Kamal's ill-mannered ass is up at the front door getting searched by security as we speak."

"Oh My God!" Simone paced the floor with big alligator tears forming in the corner of her eyes. "Where is Joey?" She was starting to hyperventilate imagining the awful scenario that was about to become a reality.

"He's talking to Prayer, but I saw him looking up at the door where Kamal is standing."

"Why is he looking at him?" Simone agonized over what the answer could be. "You think he know about Lil T?" Chari shattered Simone's world putting the final nail in the coffin for the night. "I don't know about that, but the other reason we came looking for you is that Kamal is the one they had the shoot out with earlier at the park."

"What!" Simone put her hand up to her forehead.

"Me and Prayer just heard some chicks at the front door gossiping about it." Chari spoke fast. "And you know the way hoes talk, that shit is about to be all around the club."

"Oh shit! You right, I gotta get out of here!" Simone trembled with fear. "Damn, what am I gonna do now?" The two girls paced around the Men's bathroom floor.

"Let me go see if the coast is clear." Chari peeked out the door terrified of what she might see.

Thank God there was no commotion going on. She saw Prayer and Joey ending their conversation and signaled for Prayer to come in the bathroom so they could somehow get Simone out the club without drawing attention to her or them. Time was ticking and the trio had to come up with a plan quick.

BINGO! They could sneak out the back emergency exit to safety. Prayer went to ask the manager if he would do her a small favor and unlock it for them. If they could make it to the truck, they would be safe. The girls didn't have time to worry about Joey and his boys. They could hold their own. Bottom line, everyone had been searched before coming inside so at least there wouldn't be any gun-play in the club.

Chapter Six

"Is the coast clear?" Simone looked around the corner of the back door exit with her shoes and purse in hand. "Is it straight? Is anybody out there?"

"Yeah it's tight, so come the fuck on and stop bullshitting!" Chari had taken complete control of the situation pulling Simone by her wrist as the two of them ran down the littered broken glass filled alley. "Prayer is driving around to the other side to swoop us!"

As much as Simone needed to move swiftly to get out of dodge, she still found time to complain about running bare foot down the short distance. The girls didn't have time to be cute and keep any overpriced, high heels on their feet. They had to keep that shit moving.

"I think I cut my baby toe on something." Simone whined as she climbed into the back of Prayer's truck lying down across the rear seat.

"Girl, fuck your toe!" Prayer peeled out, turning the corner on two wheels. "If any one of them dudes would've came to blows, the first ass that would have been stumped would've been your wanna be slick butt."

Simone couldn't help her self and just let Prayer get the last word in. She sat up and started screaming. "Listen bitch, I don't know who the…"

"Lay your dumb ass the fuck back down, before one of them clueless idiot's spot you and you get my man's new truck shot up!" Prayer cut Simone off not allowing her to get another word in. "You're too old to be still doing this teenage bullshit! I should've left you!"

Chari was bending over wiping the dirt off her feet before she slipped her shoes back on. "Simone, she's right. You could've gotten one of us killed tonight. And you still don't know if Joey is gonna be alright! You know that Kamal stays strapped!"

"Then that's on them, not me! I just hope they don't mention Lil T." Simone sucked her teeth. "My phone bill is due next week. Joey was supposed to give me some loot later on, plus a chick like me planned on getting that new fall collection of Kenneth Cole riding boots in every color. It's the wrong time of season for me to take a loss!"

Prayer had enough of hearing Simone talking shit and slammed on the brakes throwing the huge SUV in park causing her to fall on the back floor of the truck.

"What the fuck?" Simone moaned holding her head that bumped the side of the door.

"You know what? I'm bout tired of hearing your voice! Get your cold blooded callous ass out this motherfucker and find another way home!" Prayer hissed turning around to face her so called friend who was dazed.

Chari was in shock at Prayer's demands and tried to be a mediator. "Come on Prayer we both know that she's wrong ass hell, but she's still our girl. You can't just abandon her out here like that in the middle of the street."

"Oh yes the fuck I can. I could care less." Prayer clicked the door locks and frowned. "Maybe Miss Big-N-Bad can catch a ride in the ambulance that one of her damn baby daddy's will be passing by in, in a few fucking minutes!"

"Don't say that!" Chari argued at Prayer not really knowing what was taking place back at the club. "That's not nice to even say. Joey is a good guy and even though I can't stand Kamal, I don't want his evil ass hurt either."

"Yeah, don't say that bitch! Why is you hating on my hustle like that and shit!" Simone finally got her self together. "For real doe chick, stay outta mines!"

Prayer looked at Chari and smirked pointing in the back seat of the huge SUV. "You see what I mean? This simple minded trick tramp don't give two shits about nobody but her damn self! Fuck endangering innocent people! Let me hurry up and drop her no good ass off back where I found her!"

"Don't do me no favors!" Simone sat straight up in the seat with no remorse, folded arms sucking her teeth while bucking out her eyes. "I'll find a damn way to the crib and yall bitches can really stop talking about me like I ain't here!"

"Shut up both of yall!" Chari yelled with frustration banging on the dash board. "Damn shut up!"

With that exchange of words Prayer restrained her self putting the Range Rover back in drive and quickly hit a few dark remote side streets before jumping on the expressway. The ride to Simone's house was filled with silence. Prayer concentrated on the road as her mind wondered how Drake would react if he was to ever find out about the danger that Simone had put her in. Chari sat in the passenger seat dumbfounded as she imagined what would be the outcome if Kamal and Joey locked horns. She silently asked God to watch over everyone back at the club, especially Joey.

Simone wasn't the least bit worried about either man, just her game. She pulled out her cell phone and sent a text message to Joey trying to explain her sudden disappearance. The rest of the time Simone spent trying to fix her hair and search her purse for a breath mint.

Unlike the way going to the club, there was no music, no laughter and no conversation. It was like being the only night watchman down at the local morgue.

"I know this ain't the same fool from the park. It sure the hell looks like him?" Joey had the self control of a predator as he watched every move that Kamal and Big Ace made. From them getting patted down and searched,

to the coke and rum they ordered from the far side, of the crowded bar. Joey eye balled the heavy set chick with the tied zillions stuffed in the cheap red dress that Big Ace rubbed on the ass. He was so mesmerized with them he even started to mimic their mannerism forgetting all about Simone and her girls that were still M.I.A. in the bathroom.

"What's the deal dude?" Trevon snapped Joey out of his trance. "Put a brother up on game."

Joey tightened his grip around the neck of the beer bottle he was holding down at his side. His apparent anger was written across his face. "You know them Cats that was pushing them F-150's at the park?"

"Yeah what about them?" Trevon immediately became on the defensive scanning the crowded room. He bit his lower lip awaiting his friends answer.

"I think that's two of them silly ass motherfuckers posted over there." Joey nodded his head towards the far left side of the noise filled club. His teeth were clenched tightly as he spoke. "The guy over there standing near big girl in the red with the glass in her hand."

Trevon focused in on Big Ace and Kamal. As he joined his comrade in watching the dudes that were just hours earlier trying to take them out the game permanently, he grew increasingly heated. "Are you sure?"

"Yeah Tre I'm sure! The big dude was one of the fucking shooters that raised up and other homeboy with the mouth full of gold was pushing the blue truck! Trust me. That's them!"

"Dogg, I'm bout to go over there and give both of they families something to do on Saturday morning." Trevon cracked his knuckles then rubbed his chin.

Joey held his boy's shoulder trying to calm him down. He tried reasoning with him before things got out of hand. "Hold up Tre. Look around. This motherfucker is packed. Plus we got Simone and her girls with us. We ain't trying to catch no case for them cowards or gamble on getting nobody else hurt. It's a right time and place for everything." Joey raised the now warm bottle to his lips and took a swig. "Besides, them mark busters ain't seen us yet. I'm about to make a call to the rest of the fellas so they can get down here and post up at the front."

"Yeah you right Joey." Trevon frowned. "But before the night is over I'm gonna lay them fools down! I ain't gonna just let them come out to the park and gangsta us!"

"I feel you, but just chill out for a few and let me handle this. Joey reached on his waistband to get his cell phone. When he flipped it open the screen read,

"ONE MESSAGE"

He pushed the tiny envelope button on his phone and started scrolling down to retrieve the message.

"WENT HOME- STILL SICK"

Joey let out a big sigh of relief when he saw the text message from his son's mother. As much as they argued and fought like cats and dogs, he wanted to make sure that Simone was ghost and out of harm's way. *"Damn, that's one less thing in the mix to handle tonight. Simone's drunk ass would've just been in the way."*

A calculated masterminded Joey let his mind wonder all of five seconds before he placed the call to his crew. He knew he'd have to do something quick to handle things before Trevon's fury and aggression blew up and things turned haywire.

Chapter Seven

Kamal gulped his drink down as he surveyed women who walked pass. He was definitely way beyond being blasted. Coupled up with the blunt that they'd just finished and the ecstasy pill he'd popped, he was gone. "Damn you got a big booty!" Kamal slurred to one. "You wanna come home with a real big dick pimp?" He questioned another with malice.

Big Ace was a little bit more chill with his high as he pushed up on a thick chick with her huge 38 DD's damn near falling out her dress. You could tell she was out her shit too by the way she was throwing herself all on Big Ace letting him grab her ass up in both hands. She didn't know him from Adam, but that didn't matter. Kamal and Big Ace had only been inside the club for less than fifteen minutes before the female made her move. Big Ace had everything that she wanted and found attractive in a man;

an expensive iced out chain, a pocket full of dough and last but never least, a huge print bulging in his pants.

Leaning back on the bar getting a little light headed from the combination of all the chemicals in his system, Kamal reached his hand in his pocket pulling out a semi crushed pack of cigarettes. After taking one out putting it in his mouth, he fumbled around looking for his lighter.

"Hey Man, you got my shit?"

Preoccupied with the over zealous freak, Big Ace didn't hear his partner in crime. His mind was on one thing and one thing only.

"Damn Nigga, get ya hands off that nut gobbler and see if you got my fire!" Kamal was now sweating buckets looking as if he was gonna fall out.

"Why I gotta be all that?" The female screamed back with her hands planted firmly on her hips.

"You'll be whatever the fuck I say you is!" Kamal lunged at the girl who didn't flinch or blink an eye.

"Try ya luck. I ain't scared of ya crazy ass!" She giggled dismissing him as she would a fly. "Please don't play your self! You can't hardly even see straight!"

Home girl was one of them serious throwback hardcore project chicks that you only saw in the movies or read about in a good ass book. Popping gum, way too much Make up painted on and dirty feet, she ain't have shit, didn't know shit and wasn't gonna never be shit. All she wanted in life was a big dick inside her ever so often, a hot meal once or twice and a few dollars at the end of the month when shit was tight for her and her three nappy headed illegitimate bastards. Well tonight was that night and trust, this female was fearing no man! She was ready to come to blows to make sure all her flirting and talking trash paid off. She had hungry mouths at home to feed.

Big Ace stepped in the middle trying to avoid a scene and put his arm around his boy. "Listen Dude. You about done had it for the evening. Why don't we jet. We can get some grub and then you can sober up and drop me and ole girl here off at your crib so I can get my truck?"

Kamal looked the female in the red dress up and down then laughed out loud at her spunk. "I feel you my dude! This one right here is a wild cat!" He gave Big Ace some love still dissin' the chick on the humble.

"I wanna hit this hoe off with a lil something something!" Big Ace informed his boy on the sly.

Kamal's mind drifted to the thought of getting with Simone later that night. Big Ace's taste was miles different from his. This chick or none of her big boned sidekicks that were waving at him trying to get his attention could hold a candle to Simone.

"Yeah Dogg, you know how it is!" Big Ace grinned as he rubbed his manhood. "She about ready for Big Daddy!"

The female and Big Ace knew that Kamal was right. Ole girl didn't even mind Kamal's ugly spirited insults. It was all part of being *'out there'*. They both planned on getting busy later if things went right so why not cut out the preliminaries and get down to the business of freaking. Fair exchange was never a robbery. *Pink for green was her motto.*

After the female informed the rest of her sack chasing friends that she'd hit a lick and was leaving with Big Ace and his boy, the trio started making their way towards the door. Kamal stopped, looking on the other side of the room. A strange feeling came over him. He thought that he was being watched. For a brief second Kamal and Joey's sights locked across the smoke filled club. Joey was burning a hole through Kamal with his eyes.

This was gonna be it! The shit was gonna hit the fan! Simone's big concocted web of deceit was now just a matter of seconds from being exposed to both men.

Joey felt an adrenaline rush, seeing Kamal off point from all the liquor he'd watched him and his boy drink. The thought of his car being shot up, his new sneakers being fucked up and the recurring memory of the sounds of all the terrified parents and kids that were at the park earlier, caused Joey to get an instant migraine.

An intoxicated Kamal paused trying to regroup. For a hot moment in time he kinda thought he recognized the dude at the booth, Joey, but shook it off thinking that he was faded and the X had him hallucinating. "Damn, I need to get some fresh air. I'm seeing things." He took a deep breath. "I gotta get out this loud motherfucker and try to call Simone's whore ass back anyhow and see why she ain't picking up!"

☼

"Where the hell are they going so damn quick?" Joey had to physically hold Trevon back as they leered at their two nemesis approach the exit. "Why we just standing here like some suckers? They about to dip!"

"Shit, I know it's no way in hell that J-Rock, Mookie or Looney Larry is out front posted yet!" Joey rubbed his sweaty palms together.

"Fuck it! Let's roll after they asses!" Trevon broke loose.

"Come on Tre, think." Joey was about to breakdown the science that made him the leader as he stood in front of his hyper road dogg. "Do you really wanna run out this crowded witness packed motherfucker with guns blazing?" Joey raised his eyebrow as he looked at Trevon with an expression that a father would give his son. "Do you wanna be a fool that spends all his stashed money fighting a no win murder case and then sits 20-30 behind the prison walls wondering why the hell didn't I slow down and think?" He was on a roll with being the negotiator. "Your people ain't gonna put shit in your account and that calling collect crap is a wrap off jump."

Trevon grabbed a napkin wiping the perspiration off his bald head finally realizing that Joey was making sense. "I guess you right, Homeboy."

"I know I'm right!" Joey signaled for the waitress to bring another round of shots. "Let them cowards live to see one more sunrise! Just like we just peeped they ass out in this club, they'll be out and about in another spot and bet money, next time we'll be ready."

Joey called his crew back canceling his request to have the front door covered. He informed them that their targets were ghost and he'd holler later.

Joey suggested they should just continue getting buzzed and try pretending that they didn't even spot Kamal and Big Ace. And considering the fact that Simone and her girlfriends were ghost, Joey could now openly talk shit and do a little harmless flirting with Tami. He made sure to first text message his son's mother back before getting all the way loose informing her that he'd be by her house later on about one or two. For Simone, it was her lucky night so far because both of Lil T's fathers had dodged the bullet and were alive safe and sound for the time being.

Chapter Eight

☼

Prayer exited the Lodge Freeway at Livernois and made a quick right onto Dexter. She then placed her tiny sandal on the gas pedal flooring it until she saw Simone's block. It was a little after midnight, but you couldn't tell from the amount of people that were out on Richton St. It was bad enough the crackheads and drug addicts were out doing what they do, yet flat out it was no legitimate reason for small kids to still be running around, unsupervised no less, playing dodge ball under the street lights.

In front of Simone's house sitting on the curb were some of the same children that'd been outside ever since the girls had left earlier to go to the club. Prayer had to blow her horn to practically avoid hitting some of the older defiant ones. The sound of the truck's horn woke an exhausted still half drunken Simone up out of her sleep.

"Dang gee. Is we here already?" She wiped her red eyes and stretched. "That was fast as hell."

"Yeah it was pretty fast." Chari added looking back.

"Bitch, it wasn't fast enough! Now get out my man's truck and kick rocks!" Prayer snarled with her mind still focused on Simone's disrespect of human life. She hit the door locks and pushed the volume button of the radio up on high. Prayer was no longer in the mood for hearing Simone's voice or snappy one line comebacks.

Chari could tell that her friend was not trying to be bothered anymore with Simone so she just waved her hand and turned completely back around in the seat not to jeopardize her ride home.

"Oh so it's like that?" Simone cracked the door placing her right leg outside. She dropped one of her shoes on the ground and searched the floor of the truck for the other. Simone then tried yelling over the sounds that were blasting out of the speakers. "Yall sluts trying to go all hard and shit with a chick?"

After five or so seconds of waiting for a response and not getting one, Simone reached across the seat grabbing her purse and climbed out the truck. The heels of her feet barely touched the concrete before Prayer burned rubber over Simone's shoe and down the crowded block out of sight leaving her standing on the edge of the curb.

Simone bent down becoming enraged as she tried to pry her shoe's smashed heel out the ground. "That bitch." She mumbled angrily. "I outta kick her prissy ass."

All the shots she'd done at the club still had her dizzy. When she leaned up, attempting to get her self together, Simone lost her balance. The neighborhood kids laughed at her misfortune as she staggered towards her walkway. Before she could put her key in the door good Simone heard a voice yelling out her name.

"Simone! Simone!" The voice got louder and more demanding. "You hear me calling you!"

Simone rolled her eyes to the top of her head turning around to see Ms. Holmes walking down the sidewalk with Lil T in her arms. "Yes Ms. Holmes. What is it?" Simone held her composure the best she could.

"What do you mean? This is your son isn't it?"

"And? So!"

"And just what time did you plan on coming to get him from my house? Whenever you felt like it?"

"I'm just getting home. Give me a break!" Simone was slowly reaching her breaking point for the night.

"No My Dear, you give me a break and stop pawning your responsibility off on Yvette. He's your burden to bear."

"Yvette likes watching my son. Plus, I look out for her little behind."

"If you call filling her head with all type of nonsense about not needing an education to make it in the world looking out for her then by all means congratulations, you've succeeded." Ms. Holmes handed Simone her son. "Day after day I watch you and try to find some good in you, but I can't." She slowly shook her head. "It's no wonder that your own mother doesn't want any parts of you!"

That was the straw that snapped the camel's back. Simone sat a sleepy Lil T down in the lawn chair on the porch. She then placed her purse and keys in the empty flower pot. All the people outside seemed to get quiet as the main attention was now focused on the argument.

Ms. Holmes was one of the few neighbors on the block that had the awful misfortune of living in the same housing project as Simone did growing up. At one point back in the day before Simone's mother got Saved, her and Ms. Holmes played bridge and hung out together. That was then, but this was the here and now. Knowing Simone as a young girl didn't give her the right to disrespect her as a grown ass woman and not to mention on her own front steps, in front of everyone! Respect ya elders be damned, Ms. Holmes needed to be checked.

Simone felt her hand itching as she reached back all the way to Mother Africa and made contact with Ms. Holmes wrinkled face giving her the business. "Listen you rumor starting hag. I done had it up to here with you and all the commotion you keep going on this block!"

Ms. Holmes lost her footing, falling to the ground. "I'm gonna call the authorities on you and your bastard son! You've got one hell of a nerve putting your hands on me!" "You've got some nerve always going from house to house telling people's personal business. What about that?" Simone felt no kind of sympathy for Ms. Holmes whatsoever. "It's no way in hell I should know all about Mrs. Reynolds gas being shut off last week or poor old Mr. Mc Kenzie getting fired for drinking on the job."

Simone was just getting started. "Oh… son of a bitch! I almost forgot about the three abortions that Melody, the preacher's grand daughter had this year!"

Ms. Holmes was trying to get off the ground, but was receiving no help from the crowd that had gathered. She was embarrassed that all the gossip she was spreading was now coming back to bite her in the ass. Once again karma was alive and well. "Is anyone gonna help me to my feet?" She grabbed for the nearest arm, Yvette, her foster child who boldly snatched away.

The neighbors whose names that Simone shamelessly mentioned for all to hear disappeared into the dark returning to their homes to face their demons. The others lowered their heads hoping that they weren't next on the chopping block. Every Sunday church going Lori, who sucked dick for crack on the regular, Chubbs the shy stuttering midget that lived at the corner house who was Lori's best customer and even nine year old Denise, who still pissed in the bed nightly, were terrified that their secrets would be blurted out next. No one was immune to Simone's hard edge sword of insults she was swinging.

Everyone that made their way to the front of Simone's crib expecting a show got one that would definitely be the talk of the hood for several weeks to come.

"Ain't nobody out here giving a shit if you crawl your ass back to your porch!" Simone turned around picking Lil T up in her arms, flung open her door and stood stern with her son posted on her hip. "Now if you don't mind I'm about to go in *'my house'*. The one that *'I own, not rent.'*

So everyone please do me a huge favor and remove ya asses from my property before I make a call and I don't mean the fucking crooked ass police!"

Slamming the door in the faces of her stunned neighbors, Simone carried a sleepy Lil T to her room laying him across her king size bed. She had to use the bathroom and try to get her self together before she undressed him and put his pajamas on. Even with all the confusion that'd just taken place Simone was still high. What she needed more than anything else was a good nights' sleep.

Prayer turned the radio down as soon as they hit the next block over from Simone. "I can't take anymore

Chari. I gotta cut that chick out of my life once and all for good."

"I know what you mean." Chari replied. "Each time I try to deal with her and all the drama she brings, I end up getting cursed out. I just hope Joey's okay."

"Well this time is the last time for me hanging out with her. I don't know about you but I have to look out for my best interest. Simone is always running off at the mouth saying that she's strictly 'out 4 self', well A.S.A.P. so the fuck am I. I'm so over that bitch!"

"Girl, I feel you. You know I do." Chari started to preach to her friend as she reminisced about the past. "It's just the fact that when I think about the way that Simone's mother just up and did a flip flop on her, I kinda understand why she's so out cold with her shit."

"Okay, okay. Her old girl flipped out turning her back on Simone's ass. Well, boo hoo for her. I'm all cried out. We all were born in the hood with a hard luck story to tell."

Chari wasn't done trying to make excuses. "Yeah Prayer, but it wasn't like any of us seen that situation unfolding. One day Simone's mom, my mother and a couple of other women were playing cards and Ms. Harris just got up from the table and nutted up on everyone."

"Chari, trust me. I know the story, but damn!" Prayer turned the corner jumping back down on the freeway.

"If my mother turned her back on me outta the blue, just like that." Chari snapped her fingers. "I'd bug out too."

"Yet and still, her ass is still cut off. I'm done!"

"I know Prayer. I feel the exact same way. It's just that every single time I try to stay away, I miss Lil T."

"Lil T is sweet as pie, too sweet to be caught up in the middle of Simone and all her games. One day Joey or Kamal gonna wise up and ask for a blood test. Then you know what Chari, she's gonna be fucked for real!"

"For her sake and Lil T, I hope that Joey's the father."

"Yeah, you right girl. Cause to have a stupid bitch like Simone for a mother and Kamal's no good ass for a daddy will fuck a grown motherfucker up, let alone a kid."

Simone came out the bathroom with her robe on. The hot shower water spraying her worn body proved to be just what she needed after throwing up twice more. The house was silent as she walked into her bedroom seeing Lil T was still fast asleep. Taking his tennis shoes and socks off, she tossed a sheet over him and quietly closed the door. Simone decided to look out her front window and was amused and impressed with the way she had shut the block down for the night. *"I guess they all in they little sugar shacks with hurt feelings plotting on kicking Ms. Holmes square up her ass!"*

Falling back onto the couch with a content smile plastered of her face, Simone reached for the television remote with one hand and a half smoked blunt with the other. *"Damn this is what a bitch really needs."*

She was almost in total relax mode, feeling good and twisted when her cell phone rang. *"What does this psycho want now?"* Realizing that it was crazy Kamal made her start to cough and choke.

"Hello." she gagged, sniffing her nose and pressing mute.

"Where the fuck you been?"

"Huh?"

"Don't huh me Simone. I said where the fuck you been? I called your punk ass earlier and you didn't answer."

Simone coughed twice more before she could reply. "I was here stretched out on the couch." She lied playing it off. "I don't feel well. I've been sleep all evening. I took some cold medicine that has me drained."

"Oh I was about to come over there and get off into ya ass. I thought you was out in them streets giving my pussy away!" Kamal belched into the phone indicating that he'd been and still was drinking.

"Never that," Simone giggled to her self, "It's all about you and only you."

Kamal's manhood was back in tact. Simone didn't have to worry about him storming over causing a scene and taking her car out the driveway like he usually did when things didn't go his way.

"Dig dis here Baby, me and Big Ace is out doing what niggas do. When I get finish I'll be over there to hit them guts so make sure Lil T is knocked the fuck out."

Simone was stuck not knowing what to say. Glancing over at the clock she realized that it was damn near two o'clock and Joey had text her earlier telling her of his intentions to fall through also. "Shit!" She wanted to tell

Kamal that she wasn't feeling up to him coming over, but knew that he'd get suspicious and probably really kick her ass. "Yeah okay, but do me a favor and call me first so I can hear the doorbell. These pills got me exhausted." Simone knew she needed a heads up just in case Joey was still over and she had to try to rush him out the door.

"Come on now. What the fuck I look like calling my woman telling her I'm on my way. I'll be there when I get there so be listening the hell out! You heard me?"

"Yeah okay," she flipped her phone closed praying that Kamal wouldn't show up. When he was locked up the entire Lil T situation was easier to play off. Simone was no fool opening the cell back up dialing Joey's number. She was trying to cover all bases. After two rings he picked up.

"What up doe?"

"Hey Joey, what's up?" Simone was putting on her best 'Damn A Bitch Tired As Hell See You Tomorrow' routine, but he wasn't buying it.

"You Sweetheart. They just called last call for alcohol. When me and the fellas down these last two rounds I'll be on my way over so we can finish what we started."

"Baby, I'm still feeling sick as hell. I think I'm about to fall out. Just call me early in the morning."

"Don't worry. I'll stop by the 24 hour burger joint and grab you some hot tea and something to put on your stomach." Joey was genuinely concerned. "I'll be there in a few. Kiss my son for me until I get there. Peace"

"FUCK!" Simone screamed tossing her phone beside her.

This was some crazy mess that she had tangled her self up in. Feeling her heart beat increase with each minute and second that ticked by, Simone leaped to her feet and paced the floor trying to figure out a quick solution. Under any normal circumstances she could have Chari rush over no matter what time of day or night and cock block Joey or Kamal. They would get aggravated that they couldn't get loose with company in the house and jet.

This night was different. Somehow the tables had turned and Chari had all of sudden grown balls, jumped ship and was taking sides with Prayer. When she needed her the most, her doormat Chari wasn't there. Simone couldn't call either of her friends and come up with a sure fire scheme to get her up out of this bullshit that was about to jump off. They were both calling them selves pissed, so fuck em' and Yvette was totally out of the question.

   Simone's stomach was doing flip-flops causing her to rush back in the bathroom to spit up once more. "I ain't drinking shit else ever again in life," she repeated over and over as she stared into the mirror at her red puffy eyes and tighten the belt on her robe, "that's why you off your game tonight you dumb bitch!"

   It was nothing for her to do, but sit on the couch and get high waiting for what ever was gonna happen to happen. However the scenario played itself out then so be it. The whole baby daddy crap was getting on her last nerves anyway. Simone kicked her slippers off rubbing her sore feet.

   The high grade weed she was smoking had her wishing that she was Bewitched or that damn I Dream of Jeannie. That way all she had to do was twitch her nose or bob her head and she'd be somewhere chilling on an isolated tropical island instead of laid out on the couch in the heart of the ghetto waiting to get her ass kicked or killed by one or both of Lil T's fathers.

Times like this, when Simone was all alone and things were at their worse, she yearned for her mother who was not trying to deal with her at all. The last time Simone tried calling her Mom to invite her to Lil T's very first birthday party, she got hung up on. The next day when she made an attempt to call back the telephone number was changed. If that was what Being Saved meant, turning your back on your own child, then Simone was glad to be what her mother often referred to her as an *Outcast* and *Shepherd for Satan*.

After years of Simone plotting and scheming to get over she was drained of any emotional feelings in her heart.

"Whatever either one of them suckers wanna do tonight, fuck it! Let em' do it! I'm tired of playing the game!" Simone closed her weary eyelids drifting off to sleep.

Chapter Nine

Ms. Holmes slowly wobbled through the mob of furious neighbors who watched her with disgust. Some wanted to knock her back on the ground, while others just turned their noses up as she passed. Her days of sitting on the front porch back biting, gossiping and collecting stories, spreading them here and there were now over. Simone had snatched her mask off. Ms. Holmes' true identity was revealed smack dab in the middle of the street.

Everyone was now shockingly aware of the snake that they had living amongst them. The public embarrassment that Ms. Holmes intended to unleash on Simone had backfired. The tables had turned and now she was the bad guy. The people that she'd befriended now felt betrayed and used. A group beat down was the mentality of all.

When she reached her house placing her hand on the rusty railing the screws gave way causing her to slip once more scraping her knee. "This is all that no good trouble maker's fault." Ms. Holmes moaned practically crawling into her living room getting her address book from her dresser. Picking up the telephone receiver she started dialing. "I'll fix her little red wagon. She'll see!"

Yvette sat on the couch with her arms folded. Watching every single movement that her foster mother made, she clenched her teeth with remorse for not sticking up for her idol, Simone.

"Why you keep picking on her all the time?"

"Listen here young lady. Don't question me in my own house." Ms. Holmes waved the phone towards her and shouted across the room. "I don't know who in the hell you think you are. You starting to get beside yourself. After I finish dealing with that damned Simone maybe I'll call the folks at the agency about you!"

"Do what you feel." Yvette growled. "I'm done with running around here cooking and cleaning for your old self anyhow! I ain't no slave!"

"What did you just say?"

"You heard me! I don't care!"

"Get your ungrateful orphaned behind off my couch, go in the room I allow you to occupy and go to bed!" Ms. Holmes hung the phone back up momentarily as she ranted at Yvette. "I'm not playing with you either or the next call I make is really gonna be to the social worker to pick you up first thing in the morning."

Yvette reluctantly made her way to her bedroom. *"Dang gee, I wish I could go live with Simone."* After slamming the door as hard as she possibly could she took off one of her gold earrings that Simone had blessed her with and pressed her ear to the door. *"Why she hate Simone so much?"* Yvette wondered listening to Ms. Holmes dial a phone number. *"And who the hell she calling?"*

"Simone isn't any good at all. She's a terrible mother and an all out awful human. Little Terrell is left in my care days and days at a time." Ms. Holmes wasn't stretching the truth to the person at the other end of the conversation, she was out right lying through her teeth. "Sometimes that child is so filthy it takes two or three good hot baths to get some of that dirt off his behind. And that's not all. You should see the rags she dresses him in. Oh Lord have mercy, I feel sorry for that little boy." She continued without even taking a second to breathe or giving the party on the other end a chance to respond. "It's a crying shame! All I was trying to do was help and she slapped me in my face!"

The impressionable teen wanted to climb out the bedroom window and bang on Simone's door to put her hero up on exactly what Ms. Holmes was doing, but she was scared that the old bitch would keep her word and call the people on her next. *"I hate her ass! I hate her!"*

Yvette had no way of knowing that Ms. Holmes had no intentions on giving up that monthly foster care check she was receiving on her behalf. Yvette being disrespectful or not didn't matter, that income wasn't getting out of Ms. Holmes' greedy hands. She went on and on for a good twenty minutes or so non-stop before hanging up. She never shut up long enough for the other person to ask a question, leaving Yvette finally removing her ear from the door going to bed confused and worried about what sort of chaos and turmoil tomorrow would bring.

Shortly after hanging up the phone, Ms. Holmes finally found time to put anti-bacterial crème on her knee and went into her room climbing in the bed for the night.

Chapter Ten

Kamal and Big Ace were just finishing up with cheese burger deluxe platters that they ordered. Big Ace had his arm around Monique, the girl from the club. She wasn't like the fellas, ordering a top of the line porterhouse steak and scrambled eggs. Since Big Ace was treating she decided to push the shit to the limit.

"Damn big girl! You gonna eat all of that?" Kamal tore off a small piece of the menu and picked some meat out from between his teeth. "That's why ya ass swollen now!"

"Stay out my business!" Monique screamed at him resting back in Big Ace's grip. "I still look good. Don't I Baby?"

Big Ace had already spent a few dollars on the greedy trick and didn't want to sour the deal so he quickly agreed with her. "Girl, come on! You know you the shit. It's more of you to love." He kissed her on the cheek.

"That's what I'm talking about." Monique hissed twisting her lip at Kamal. "So dig that fly shit!"

"Man, control your big bitch!" Kamal cracked a smile after spitting the loosened meat particle on the restaurant floor. "She straight outta line."

Monique wasn't done yet. "Why you here chilling with us? Where's your bitch at anyhow?"

Kamal raised his shirt revealing his gun which was tucked nicely in his waistband. "This right here is my bitch! Now what you know about this?"

"Oh, it's all good for me!" Monique's voice became sarcastic in tone as she rubbed on Big Ace. "I like my shit hard black and shiny! And I guess you do too, huh?"

"Oh you's one of them smart mouth big bitches!" Kamal spit out another small piece of meat, "I'm all Man. Ain't nothing soft about this right here!"

Monique was still persistence. "Alright then, I ain't mad at ya! I'm just saying, you want me to call one of my girls to hang out with us?"

Kamal looked her dead in her face and burst out laughing. "You mean one of them skank dust bunnies you was running with back at the club? You've gotta be out your mind for even saying that crazy shit!"

"What's wrong with my girls? You think you too good to roll with them or something?"

Big Ace had to join in on his boy's defense. "Monique, I ain't trying to front for ole boy here," pointing at Kamal "and no disrespect, but you are the pick of the litter."

"Yall ain't shit!" She rolled her eyes as she reached for the desert menu. "I'm getting this to go."

"Damn, ya ass still hungry?" Kamal rubbed his chin as he pulled out his cell phone.

"Didn't I tell you to mind your own?" Monique fumed.

"It's all good. I'm about to call my son's mother anyway. Maybe if you play your cards right with Big Ace I'll let my girl take your wide ass to the gym with her!"

The fellas laughed as Monique sucked her teeth still checking out the menu. Kamal pushed redial and Simone's name which was locked in blinked in the screen. Big Ace signaled the waitress so they could break camp.

"Come on Tre. You about ready to dip or what?" Joey stood up calling Tami over to settle up his tab that he'd started. "I got business to tend to."

"Yeah, I'm bout ready." Trevon answered waving a chick over that he'd met on the dance floor. "Just let me tell this female where to meet me at outside."

Joey paid Tami what he owed plus a little bit more. She wrote her number down on a napkin and gave it to him. Making it crystal clear that she was open and available when and if he was free. Joey took the number, but knew he never planned on using it. Drunk or not. Bossy or not. Bitch or not. Simone was his girl and he loved her to death. It was no way that he would or could just dis her like that. Fun was fun, but the night of games was over and it was time to go home and tend to his sick Wifey.

After the house lights came on Joey and his crew made their way towards the door. After a lot of handshakes and politicking they were in front of the club. Trevon was now with the chick and climbing into his ride. The hotel was their next stop of the night.

Joey, of course flying solo, had to swing by the all night joint and grab some grub before going to his final destination for the night… Simone's.

☼

Kamal hung up his cell phone slightly grinning. "Her ass know what time it is!"

"Who was that? Simone?"

"Yeah that was her." Kamal licked his lips. "She over at the crib sick. That's why she ain't pick up earlier." He was happy to offer his friend an explanation considering the way he'd bugged out before at the spot.

"Oh dig that!" Big Ace was skeptical about Simone's flimsy excuse, but shrugged his shoulders not really caring one way or the other.

"Who is Simone?" Monique butted in.

"That's my Baby Momma!" Kamal sat back stretching his arms. "The one that can give ya wild ass some tips on dressing!"

"Who you talking about, Simone Harris that used to live near me?"

"It depends where you live at," Kamal fired back, "with ya Inspector Gadget ass!"

"I live around the way at the Truth Homes." Monique said proudly without hesitation.

"Oh you mean the fucking projects?"

"Yeah so?"

"Whoa!" Big Ace threw his hands up. "Calm down with all the loud talk. I was born in them projects too."

"I'm sorry Sweetie." Monique hugged on him. "But ya boy been tripping all night and shit. I'm tired of his mouth. When we gonna bounce?"

Big Ace went in his pocket revealing a knot causing Monique's pussy to drip at the sight. He paid the bill and they were out the door making their way to the crowded parking lot. Kamal suddenly stopped glaring vindictively at Willy Dale, the local begging bum, slumped over on the side of the restaurants wall with a dirty cup clutched in his hand. The late night regular customers were blessing him with spare change and empty bottles out their cars.

Making his way closer to Willy Dale, Kamal raised his left Tim, kicking the less than fortunate man's hard earned revenue across the lot causing him to crawl around like a baby trying to recover all the cup's contents. "Damn Dogg! Why you do that bullshit to ole Willy Dale?" Big Ace asked confused about his boy's actions.

"Man, fuck his homeless ass! I ain't got no love for these annoying motherfuckers out in these here streets!"

"You wrong as hell!" Monique dug in her purse revealing the fact for the first time all night that her mooching ass actually had a couple of dollars.

"Oh dig that!" Kamal called her out to Big Ace changing the subject. "Her wide ass been holding out. This hoe got a pocket full of dough! She should've been treating us!"

Big Ace was tired of Kamal and all his foolish behavior. He put his arm around Monique walking her off into the direction of the truck. She had her carry out bag in her hands and Big Ace's money on her mind.

Climbing her mostly breast overweight body into the back cab of the truck she mean mugged the back of Kamal's head as he pulled out the lot thinking about just how dumb he was. She wanted to just haul off and slap him on the back of his neck, but she chilled.

"I ain't even gonna put that nigga up on game."

Monique's mind jumped back to the club. If her eyes weren't playing tricks on her from drinking too much, she was almost certain that she'd seen Ms. 'think she better than everyone else that still live in the projects' Simone posted at a booth with Joey, the dude she thought was Simone's baby daddy. Monique knew for a fact that Simone's home girls, Chari and Prayer were definitely in the house. She almost had a run in with the bitches in the middle of the night club, but they asses knew better and kept that shit on the high post move.

Monique started to giggle settling in the seat. *"Now this trying to go for hard, cock blocking Negro, wanna throw salt in my game. As much as I hate Simone I would put him up on the bullshit, but considering how he acts, he got the shit coming. For real for real, I'm glad she giving his ass the straight up motherfucking business! Forget even telling his rude ass that Simone is playing him! Good for her!"*

Kamal was on his way to get on the freeway. He positioned his seat back getting comfortable for the long drive across town.

"Hey fat girl in the back seat, don't forget to strap them big titties of yours down. I don't need them gigantic twins slapping me on the back of my head while I'm driving!"

"Go fuck yourself!" Monique shouted. *"Good for her!"*

"Damn Dude, shut up with all that madness we get the point!" Big Ace interjected fed up with Kamal's mouth. Kamal knew his boy was heated and floored it so he could hurry up dropping Big Ace and Monique off at Big Ace's truck. Then he would double back and sleep at Simone's.

Joey did a triple take getting a quick glance of a royal blue F-150 going down the freeway ramp as he was coming up. *"Naw, couldn't be."* He reasoned with his self unknowingly turning into the 24 hour restaurant that Kamal had just moments earlier left. No sooner than he stepped out, he ran into a couple of females that were out hanging at the park when all the commotion jumped.

"What's up Joey?" Karen shyly flirted.

"Oh hey Karen. What it do?"

"Just up here getting a sandwich to take home." She winked her eye. "You know how it go."

Karen was one of those not so attractive females that had to go the extra mile to get a brother to notice her so she always made it known that she was easy and had no problem with paying like she weighed.

"Yeah I feel you." Joey acknowledged her pimping backing up slightly not to encourage her.

"I'm glad you and your boy's are alright from that stuff out at the park." Karen twirled her extra long weave with her fingers still trying to push up on Joey.

"Yeah Karen, that was some pretty fucked up shit!"

"It really was." She agreed. "Two of them lunatics and Money Making Moe just left this bitch."

"Is Monique still out here setting folks up?"

"Come on Joey. You know how she roll."

"Well dig, I need to get this food and be out. I'll holler!"

Joey saw a frantic Willy Dale over on the edge of the curb chasing a crumbled up dollar bill as he stepped inside. Any other time he would've given him a few bucks, but his mind was preoccupied. He couldn't believe what he'd just heard from Karen. First them busters were at Bookies, then at the restaurant. It was like they were all connected at the hip all of a sudden. He pulled out his cell phone calling Trevon with the quickness. "Hey Tre, you not gonna believe this bullshit!"

"What's the deal Homie?"

"Guess what. Those guys was just up here."

"Up where?" Trevon questioned. "Where you at?"

"I'm up here at The Midtown Grill grabbing Simone's sick behind some food."

"Is they still there? Did they see you?" Trevon was busy throwing his white tee back on. Him and the girl he'd met at the club were already half undressed chilling at the hotel. They were just about to crack a bottle of Moet that he copped from the after hours spot over on Linwood.

"Slow ya roll killer. They broke camp just before I got here." Joey laughed. "Karen's shady ass told me."

"Oh I was about to say!"

"Yeah I know, but dig what else she told me."

"What's that?"

"Man them cats is dumber than I thought. They hanging with Monique's clip-n-dip ass."

"Ahhh…hell naw!!!" Trevon motioned for the female to go ahead and open the champagne. "If I didn't wanna put some hot lead up in they grimey asses, I'd kinda feel sorry for them. Monique and her peoples don't fuck around when it come to getting that shit how they live!"

"Dogg, I feel you. Cause that bitch be on some other type of shit." Joey stated as he walked up to the carry out counter. "If Monique has her way, we ain't gotta do shit but sit back and let that bitch and her crew risk catching that case."

"Well call me if you need me. I'm about to get off into this right here!" Trevon rubbed on the girl's thigh.

"All right then, Peace!" Joey slipped his cell back on his hip and placed his order making sure to get a slice of the sweet potato pie that Lil T loved so much. As he sat patiently on the stool spinning around he kept wondering exactly why the dude with the gold fronts seemed so familiar. *"I can't remember for shit where I seen that coward from."*

Ten more minutes, Joey's number was called indicating that his food was ready. He paid the cashier, double checked his order was correct and strolled out the door heading towards his car. As Joey started his engine, Karen made sure she made her presence known by waving her hands around like she was in a freaking parade. He blew the horn twice at her and handed a grateful Willy Dale some spare change before speeding out the parking lot and into traffic.

"Stay up Old Timer!"

"Thank you Youngblood!" Willy Dale yelled out into the wind at Joey. "I appreciate ya'!"

Jazz music softly playing on the radio eased Joey's trouble filled mind. The night was about to come to an end just the way he liked it to, in the presence of his first born, Lil T. Seeing his perfect sleeping face, made Joey forget any foul shit going on in the outside world. Drug deals, drive-bys, bitches, hoes and anything other than Elmo and Big Bird mattered when it came to his seed.

So with Lil T's pie, Simone's beef and broccoli soup and fresh warm pita bread in tow, Joey's next stop would shortly be her front door. It was time to relax. Time for family, his family.

Chapter Eleven

Simone was in a deep coma like sleep. All her worries and fears of what was to come were temporarily put to rest. With her subconscious mind taking over, Simone was visiting a place that she hadn't been in years. The setting was all too familiar. Her mother was in the kitchen with an apron on. The small one bedroom project apartment was bursting at the seams. Simone's mother, as always had the crowd going by singing old Motown songs while she deep fried catfish and puffed on a joint.

You could tell it was the first of the month because all the normally depressed low income tenants had just received their food stamp benefits and were in the party mood. It was nothing like getting your check or some stamps to get someone's quiet ass to get the Holy Ghost.

The second hand half price stereo blasted sounds of Stevie Wonder, Diana Ross, Smokey Robinson and The

Temptations. With two card games going on and plenty of food and drink, it would be damn near daybreak before the monthly get together would let up.

Simone, Chari and some of the other project children danced around showing off their best moves. The spur-of-the-moment contest winners would receive anything from a dollar bill to a sip of beer. The grown ups would do just about anything to keep their kids quiet so they could keep the party going as long as possible. Everyone loved everyone and that made the atmosphere perfect.

Ms. Harris had Simone trained. She was pulling double duty serving plates, emptying ash trays and bossing around the other children. The fact that Simone was a few years younger than some of them didn't matter one bit. Her mother made sure that Simone knew everything that went on in the world so nothing would come as a shock. When the evil lady that lived on the second floor got even more malicious, Simone was the first one to point out the fact that she must've been going through menopause.

The fact that her mother treated her like an equal made Simone feel on top of the world. To her it was no better feeling than to get respect from her Mom. It was her and Simone against the world. It seemed as if they lived in a fancy castle up on a hilltop above everyone else in town. The nights the pair would spend watching old spooky movies and grubbing on food that one of Ms. Harris' many admirers would bring by, were the best times in Simone's young life.

Now that Simone's mother had did a 1-80, turning her life over to the Lord cutting all ties with anything that her church deemed unholy, Simone and her bastard son, Lil T were left on the outside looking in. But she still had her memories and it was those memories that Simone kept with her that caused her justifiably paranoid self to sleep like a baby even though shit was about to get ugly.

Joey pulled up in front of Simone's house and reached in the back seat grabbing the food. With a huge smile of contentment on his face he made his way up the walkway and onto the front porch. Every step he took had him feeling as if he was being watched. He glanced back over his shoulder. Joey's hands were filled, but he started wishing that he'd remembered to get his pistol out of his stash box underneath the passenger seat.

Realizing that the always populated block was deserted gave him an eerie chill as he knocked on Simone's door repeatedly. Even at three o'clock in the morning her block was jumping so seeing it take the form of a ghost town was strange as hell to Joey. He had no way of knowing that just about a hour or so ago his son's mother had shut the entire motherfucker down.

Without getting a response, Joey sat the bags on the lawn chair and took his cell phone off his hip dialing Simone's number. *"What's taking her silly ass so long?"* After the fifth ring, a sleepy voiced Simone answered.

Joey could hear her turning the locks on the huge solid steel door. After the last lock turned, the door seemed to have been opened by the wind as Simone walked away not even greeting him. She threw her body back on the couch and balled up like an infant trying to get back to sleep and where she left off at. Her dreams always seemed so real. It was the only time that the hardcore bitter Simone would be able to visit her mother and feel truly loved and cared for unconditionally and she wasn't in the mood for Joey to stop that emotion. Simone missed her mother and would do almost anything to make things right again.

The fact that part one of her dangerous equation had just came into her home didn't seem to phase her one bit. Simone had unfinished business with her mother. Lil T's two fathers controlled most of her days, but her dreams belonged to her and her alone.

"What took you so long Baby, I told you I was coming sleepy head? How you feeling?" Joey went into the kitchen placing the bags onto the counter. "I'll fix your food for you. That way you don't have to get back up."

He opened up the cupboard taking out a bowl and a small saucer. Joey then poured his son's mother a warm cup of tea and put her meal on a tray. When he got back in the living room, Simone was once again knocked out. Joey smiled as he watched the slobber form in the corner of her mouth. *"This is the only time your annoying pretty ass ain't begging."* He reflected to him self while caressing her soft cheek.

Placing Simone's food tray on the coffee table in front of her, Joey quietly went back into the kitchen getting Lil T's pie. It was in a plastic container looking too perfect to be touched. He held it in his hands as he tip-toed to his son's room. Slightly pushing the door open, he noticed that Lil T wasn't in his bed. Joey's face filled with disappointment. His first thought was to wake Simone up to march her behind across the street to Yvette's to get his son, but remembered that she was claiming to be sick.

  Turning around to go back in the front of the house, Joey heard tiny snoring sounds from Simone's bedroom. Peeking inside, he found his first born curled up in the same position as his mother. He stood there watching him sleep as he'd just done Simone. Joey couldn't wait until Lil T got old enough to go shoot hoops at the park with him or toss a football around. He was Joey's pride and joy. His number one priority in life was providing for his son and making sure he stayed safe.

 Being careful not to make any noise to disturb him, Joey proudly displayed the huge healthy piece of pie on the nightstand and softly kissed his son goodnight. "Sleep good Daddy's little man." He whispered. "Daddy loves you more than life."

Closing the door behind him, Joey came back into the living room where he found Simone sitting up wiping her eyes trying to focus on the light in the room.

"Oh My God! What time is it?" She alarmingly leaped to her feet mistakenly knocking the food on the floor. Reality had set back in when she realized that her other baby daddy, Kamal was probably minutes if not seconds away. "What the fuck is the matter with your crazy ass?" Joey threw his hands up in the air demanding an answer.

Kamal was less than ten minutes away from reaching Big Ace's truck. They'd run into an accident on the way making a twenty minute trip turn into double that. Enduring plenty of gawkers, several police cars and a few ambulances the exit was coming into view. Kamal looked over to his right quickly noticing that his boy, Big Ace had his head tilted back and was knocked the fuck out. After a survey of the back seat via the rear view mirror, Kamal saw the complete opposite.

"Damn, your good sack chasin' ass is hanging ain't you?"

"Chill on all that madness Kamal. Why you all on a bitch back so fucking hard and shit?"

"My bad!" He made eye contact with her in the mirror. "I thought a hoe like you liked a Nigga on ya back hard!" Monique was sick and tired of Kamal's mouth and was overjoyed when he came up top and off the freeway. Big Ace was sleep so there was no one to referee the two.

"The way you talking makes me think you jealous!"

"Jealous of what?" Kamal laughed.

"You act like you want some of this!"

"Some of what? I don't like fat meat!"

"Oh so you like them boney like Ms. Thang you fuck with huh?"

"What's it to ya ass what the fuck I like!"

"I'm just saying, that's all!"

Monique knew that Kamal was watching her so she pulled out her two secret weapons that always worked on a man. She grabbed both of her breast squeezing them together firmly. When she made sure that Kamal was good and mesmerized by the sight she stuck out her wet tongue revealing a diamond stud piercing. Monique then started to lick across her nipples while still caressing them tight.

"Do your girl Simone got it like this?" She teased flicking her tongue around.

Kamal made sure that Big Ace was still sleep before he responded. "Damn bitch! I ain't gonna front. That's some freaky shit and you got a nigga's dick hard as a motherfucker, but you about to get with my Mans here."

"See that's where you wrong. We can all party. I can handle both of yall at the same time." Monique did the same thing that Kamal had just done, check to see if Big Ace was sleep. "I like it like that!" She continued trying to convince him knowing that she'd get double pleasure and double pay."

The huge F-150 hit a pothole causing Big Ace to open his eyes and cut the sexually charged conversation short. Monique slipped her breast back into her dress before Big Ace got a chance to look at her.

"What's taking so long?" He stretched out his arms and cracked the window to get some fresh air to wake him all the way up.

"Damn Dude, you was knocked out." Kamal sneakily stumbled over his words. "It was an accident blocking that motherfucker!"

"Yeah Sweetie, you slept through all of it." For the first time all night, Monique cosigned with Kamal. "It was touch and go traffic for about three or four miles."

"Oh dig that. Shit, I'm just glad we here. I done rested up. Now a nigga ready to hang for the rest of the night!"

Kamal made a left turn into The Crestwood Apartment Complex and pulled next to Big Ace's truck.

"Alright then Dude, go do you." Kamal gave his boy some love as he watched Monique squeeze her breast once more behind Big Ace's back. "Fuck this bitch extra hard for me! Maybe in the mouth or something. That way you can shut her the fuck up for once all night!"

"Why don't you come do it yourself?" Monique hissed back. "Or are you man enough to handle all of this?"

"Damn, is yall still talking shit?" Big Ace interjected.

Kamal watched Monique's wide ass climb down out his truck and into Big Ace's. *"Her backside is hot."* Even though she was far from being the type of female he usually found attractive he would still fuck the dog shit out the tramp from the back. Kamal's manhood started to throb at the thought of what his boy, Big Ace was about to experience. He blew the horn twice at them as they drove off headed towards a hotel to get their freak on.

With a hard dick in his pants, Kamal sped off anxious to get over to Simone's house. *"I'm gonna really give her something to be sick about!"* He bent a few corners and jumped down on the expressway, hit 80 and put the F-150 on cruise control.

Chapter Twelve

Joey stood stone faced waiting for Simone to answer his question. Watching her act frantic and showing no form of concern for her precious new carpet that now had big chunks of beef and broccoli on it caused Joey to ask her the same thing. "I said what in the hell is your problem?"

"I just had a nightmare, that's all." Simone tried her best to calm down. "It was kinda scary."

"Oh is that all?" Joey bent over picking up the bowl, spoon and a few pieces of the meat. "And you knock over all the dang gone food I bought for you!"

Simone agonized staring at the digital clock that was flashing brightly on her DVD Player. *3:31…3:31…3:31.* The light was blinking repeatedly as if it was calling out to her. *3:32…3:32…3:32.* Simone's heart seemed to be beating in perfect rhythm with constant glow. *3:33…3:33.*

"Kamal is probably on his way! Naw, maybe he changed his mind! Damn what am I gonna do? Oh shit!"

"Do you hear me talking to you?" Joey looked up at Simone. "Are you deaf or something crazy girl?"

"Yeah I heard you. I was just thinking about my dream."

"Don't you mean nightmare?"

"Whatever Joey!" Simone rolled her eyes.

"Whatever my ass!" Joey screamed back shocking Simone into reality. "Is your deranged looking behind gonna help me clean this mess up or what?"

"It can wait for a minute can't it?"

"Alright then, but don't be bitching later when this crap leave a stain cause I ain't buying your ass no new carpet so you can just forget about it."

Simone had bigger things about to jump off at any fucking moment. A couple of years worth of scheming, manipulating and careful planning was all about to fall apart. She had to get prepared for the inevitable. The vein in her neck was bulging and the room started to spin.

Joey took notice of Simone's demeanor and stopped what he was doing to show her some attention. Taking his time to hold both of her hands, with affection he pulled her close to him. "Was it that bad?"

Joey ran his fingers through Simone's long hair trying to get her to relax. For a brief second Simone wanted to blurt out the truth and confess. Joey didn't deserve to be ambushed by all the madness that was coming, but what else could she do. It was against the Player's Code of Ethics to actually drop your hand and expose your own secrets. No matter how tight shit was, that damn sure wasn't an option.

"I think it was all that liquor I drank." She tried to shake the uneasiness putting back on her game face. "Maybe I should go to bed and just get some rest."

"Yeah, you right!" Joey agreed taking some of the mess to the kitchen. "In the morning you'll feel better."

"Oh shit! This nigga about to jet! Hell yeah!" Simone's mind took control. "3:40…3:40…Damn hurry up!"

When Joey came out the kitchen he had his shirt thrown over his shoulder. Simone took her eyes off the clock doing a double take at Joey. "What's up Baby? I thought you was about to go home."

He gave Simone a strange look and laughed at her off the wall crazy middle of the night comments.

"Girl, it's late as hell. I'm tired as shit. A nigga like me about to lay down next to my son and fall the fuck out!"

"What!" She objected loudly.

"I said I'm about to crash with Lil T."

As almost on cue after the last word came out of Joey's mouth, Simone's stomach bubbled and she threw up everywhere. Joey instantly jumped back just in time to avoid getting soiled.

"Your ass don't need to drink shit ever again in life!"

"I'm sorry." Simone's hand was full of a clear mixture of a slimy discharge. She trembled as she ran towards the bathroom trying not to gag again.

Joey paced the floor outside the door watching his woman once again on her knees blessing the Porcelain God. It had been a long night and he'd had about enough of Simone's over dramatic behavior. "I'm out. I'll be in the bedroom sleep when you get yourself together."

Simone got off the cold floor trying to stall him when a musical sound rang out scaring the shit out of her. Simone bumped her head on the sink. *"Oh dang!"*

It was Joey's cell phone that was on the kitchen counter. She suspiciously peeked around the corner listening closely as he answered the late night call. "You bullshitting!...Oh yeah!...Where you at?...I got you!...Sit tight?...What room?…I'm on my way!" Simone ran back into the bathroom turning the water on in the sink trying to act nonchalant and uninterested.

Joey sat his phone back on the counter as he wrote down the room number the person had given him on a piece of paper. He went back into the living room and grabbed his car keys. "Simone, I gotta go handle this situation. I'll holler at you tomorrow some time!"

Simone was happy that he was about to leave, but still had the nerve and audacity to be nosey and jealous. "Who the fuck was that?" With her hands on her hips she demanded a response. "And don't say your Momma!"

"I ain't got no time to get into with you." Joey turned the doorknob heading outside. "I'll put you up on the shit tomorrow!"

As Joey sped off in a rush to who knows where, Simone felt her blood pressure go back down to normal. She shut the door and went to clean her self up hoping that Kamal was some where passed the fuck out.

After a long look in the mirror, Simone thought out loud. *"Son of a bitch, that was close as a motherfucker! I gotta get my shit together. I'm slipping on my pimping and I'm way too pretty for all this stress these mark busters is causing me! That's probably why a hoe gaining all this extra weight! I need to cut one of them tricks loose!"*

Simone got a hot pail of water and a few rags. She then got down on her hands and knees so that she could try to scrub the spot where the spilled food was starting to soak in. As she squirted a small amount of all-purpose cleaner her eyes started to water and the smell made her feel nauseated. *"This is some foul shit! Who told Joey's, always trying to do something ass, to bring this garbage in my house any fucking way!"*

Big Ace and Monique drove in the parking lot and checked in at the Red Roof Inn on Dequindre and I-696. It wasn't the Ritz Carlton, but it wasn't a hole in the wall either. It would be 100% different if Monique was a straight up dime piece, then Big Ace would've served the bitch up wifey style instead of low budget.

The night was quiet and hushed until the pair got there. After making a gang of noise on the way to their room, Monique took the room key opening up the door. She held Big Ace's hand practically dragging him to the bed. Pushing him backwards, climbing on top, the top heavy female shoved her breast in his face. Big Ace then took it upon him self to suck on each one simultaneously.

Monique ran her tongue across his neck licking and sucking like there was no tomorrow. When she worked her way down to his muscular chest and stomach she suddenly stopped and started massaging his manhood.

"Hey Baby. Why don't you go take a hot shower and clean him up good so I can sing him a lullaby?"

"Yeah, I feel you." Big Ace happily leaped up. "Just be ready and naked for daddy when he gets back!"

"Ummm...I can hardly wait!" Monique moistened her lips while hiking up her dress to reveal her red panties.

Big Ace hurried up disappearing into the bathroom, shutting the door behind him. He was to geeked.

"*Hell yeah!*" He thought unfastening his belt. "*I'm about to bang that bitches lights out!*"

Hearing his pants hit the floor and making sure that the water in the shower was turned on, Monique grabbed her cell phone placing an important call.

"Hey it's me…Yeah…We at the Red Roof…He's in the shower…I know the routine…I got you…just hurry!"

She put her phone on silent ring then back in her purse tossing it on the night stand. With a huge smile, Monique undressed then spread eagle butt asshole naked on the king size bed awaiting Big Ace's return.

Trevon was just getting good and relaxed. The female he was with was giving him the royal king treatment. She had filled the hotel's ice bucket with warm soapy water and was washing his feet and sucking them dry. With a blunt hanging in the corner of his mouth and a triple x porno playing on the television, Trevon was in true pimp player heaven. "Why don't you crawl up here and bless me with some of them brains?"

"Yesss…Daddy…" She blushed while obeying.

Quickly obliging to serve her king for the night, the sex driven chick really made her presence felt and blessed his mic. With every deep throat gulp of his dick, his toes curled. Switching back from the movie to reality was causing him to be on the verge of a super nut. The only thing that was stopping that wonderful feeling was the distracting noises of two loud voices that were outside in the courtyard.

Frustrated, Trevon pushed the female off his hard dick and slipped back on his pants. He cracked the door and leaned over the balcony. *"It couldn't be!"*
Watching the loud obnoxious pair enter room 117, Trevon ran back in calling his boy to inform him.
"Hey Joey…I know it's late…You ain't gonna believe this!...Red Roof…Just now…Room 117…I'll be waiting."

Trevon gave the confused girl cab fare plus a little extra and sent her on her way. Even though she wanted to have her turn being treated like royalty, the unexpected money definitely made things all good in the hood for her.

No more than fifteen minutes within the girl leaving and him watching Big Ace's and Monique's room like a hawk, Trevon peeped out a car with it's headlights turned off pull in and park on the far side of the lot. Three dudes got out putting on Halloween mask.

"What the fuck?" He mumbled under his breath watching the drama unfold. "Ain't this some shit?"

   Trevon was stunned as the trio systematically inched toward room 117. He wanted to scream across the lot to the late night creepers and tell them that Big Ace's hoe ass belonged to him and his boy.

"Let me see how all this madness is about to play out."
He dialed Joey's number again to put him up on the latest developments but unfortunately got his voice mail.
"I hope ole boy ain't close to this joint yet."

   Trevon didn't want his boy driving in on the middle of whatever was going down, possibly a shootout, so he continued to watch the seemingly well executed plan jump off and would try hitting Joey back again in a few and hopefully next time he'd pick up.

Chapter Thirteen

Kamal saw Linwood Avenue and bent the corner. Crossing the railroad tracks around the curb his mind drifted back to his childhood and how fucked up shit was for him and his sister back in the day……………

"Hey Kamal. Why don't you go down to the gas station and see if you can pump some gas for a few dollars?" His drug addict Old Dude was taking his last sip of Wild Irish Rose and would soon need another and a rock of crack. "Yeah, that's a good idea!" His Mom agreed quickly when realizing that they were out of 'Get High Funds'. "Matter of fact, take your little sister there with you and let her ask all the dudes. She's developing now so I know them old men will throw her some change or a few bottles."

"Why do I have to go do that?" Kamal argued. "All my friends be laughing at me."

"Me too." La Tonya pouted. "They be making fun of us saying we be poor and dirty all the time!"

Kamal grew heated. "Yeah and I'm tired of that!"

"So fucking what? Get yall ungrateful asses up and do what the hell I told yall to do!"

"What we got to be grateful for?"

"What you just say?"

"You heard me!" Kamal's voice raised in volume.

His drunken father got up from the fabric torn musty smelling chair and back handed his son against the empty china cabinet. Kamal's lip started to bleed as he tried to protect him self from his father's wrath. Several closed fist later, Kamal decided he'd had enough and swung back with all his might. The emotional force behind the blow knocked his father unconscious.

La Tonya, his sister had tears of joy flowing down her face that her big brother finally found the courage to stand up for him self and her. But at the same time she shed tears of uncertainty, knowing that when their boozed sperm donor woke up and got his bearings, Kamal would really be in for it.

To make matters worse, the children's mother never lifted a hand or opened her mouth to stop what was going on in front of her eyes, which were already stretched open from being on a crack attack. "Well Kamal, just don't stand there looking all stupid and shit! He ain't dead or nothing!" She yelled out. "Now go on up there and see if you can get your Momma some money real quick before he wakes up and tries to drink it all up!"

"But Momma…"

"But Momma what? Now go!" She insisted.

The pain of that day still haunted Kamal after all these years. He remembered refusing his mothers demands and instead packing his belongings, which amounted to little of nothing, saying good bye to La Tonya and going out into the world to try to survive on his own. At that very moment Kamal became a man and made due. Any place was better than how he was forced to live at home.

Leaving his young sister home alone with two alcoholic junkies as parents didn't feel right to him so Kamal made a decision in her best interest placing a call Protective Services to come out and investigate the living conditions. He found out weeks later from one of the guys in the hood that the agency had swiftly stepped in doing their job, removing a suffering La Tonya from the household placing her in foster care. When they showed up to rescue her, she practically ran jumping up in their arms.

Kamal often wondered exactly where she was at and if she was being properly taken care of, but considering the fact that he was still himself just a minor, contacting the people down at Protective Services would only cause him to get caught up and become apart of the system and that wasn't an option for him. Kamal would rather tough things out and take his chances roaming the murderous crime filled streets of Detroit than be bounced from home to home in search of acceptance from strangers.

As Kamal's truck approached the Davison intersection, the blinding high beam headlights flashing from a car, which coincidently was Joey's, going in the opposite direction and a couple of loud horns blowing, brought him out of his grief packed flashback trance. Reminiscing about his treacherous upbringing almost caused him to veer over into the on coming traffic and crash.

"Shit! That was close!" He rubbed his chin ignoring the other late night drivers giving him the finger and turned on Simone's block and up to her house. Pulling in the driveway and jumping down out his vehicle, he went on the porch banging loudly twice on her front door. *"I need to piss. This tramp better hurry the fuck up!"*

When it took Simone longer than he wanted it to Kamal unzipped his pants spraying her front lawn like he was a wild dog off his leash. Before he could finish behaving so rudely, Simone flung open the door to let him in and witnessed first hand, once again, how low and unpolished Kamal really was.

"What's wrong with you? Why would you do some old stupid shit like that?" She argued. "Why didn't you go around to the backyard at least?"

"Bitch who the fuck you talking to like that?" Kamal took his hand mashing Simone's weary face backing her out his way as he came inside the house. "I done told you about that smart ass mouth piece of yours!"

Simone had already been catching hot fire hell all day and chose not to stretch the no win disagreement out. She pushed the door shut not even bothering to lock it and sat on the couch. Considering the fact that she'd played sick earlier on the phone with him she had to keep the game going. "I still don't feel good Kamal!" She whined, grabbing for her blanket wrapping it around her as if she was an Indian. "I think I have the flu or something like that."

"Oh yeah?" Kamal marched through the house suspiciously inspecting every inch. "Why is this big ass wet spot here?"

"I threw up some food that's all."

"I thought your lying ass was so sick! Where the hell did you get some food from?" Kamal got a glance of some carry out bags thrown on the kitchen counter. It was his time to catch her up in her lies and beat that ass proper. "Prayer brought it over for me on her way home from work and dropped it off." Simone passed the ball back over to Kamal. Mentioning Prayer always got him heated and off his square. "She knew I was sick and thought about a sista's health." Simone rolled her eyes at Kamal.

"What the fuck that's suppose to mean?"

"What you mean, what it mean!"

"Just what I said bitch!"

"Nothing! Just that she cared!" Simone stood her ground with the lie knowing that on the for real side of the game, Prayer, at this point, didn't care if she coughed up a lung.

Kamal was tired of hearing Prayer's name and quickly changed the subject. "My dick been rock hard as a motherfucker all night. Go get in the bed so I can get some of that pussy or did ya girl Prayer take care of that too?"

"Why you gotta act so dumb all the time?" Simone leered at him with disgust. "Didn't ya Momma teach ya any better?"

Kamal froze in his tracks. "Simone, I'm not playing with ya ass. I done told ya more than once to keep my peoples names out ya mouth!" He yanked her off the couch. "Now come on and give me some!"

"I told you I was sick. Plus Lil T is in my bed!"

"So throw his ass in his own damn bedroom!"

"Kamal, why don't you be quiet? It's late and I don't wanna wake him up." Simone put her finger up to his lips in an effort to shut him up.

Kamal snatched her wrist squeezing it tight. "Well okay then, we can do it right here!"

Simone smelt the liquor on his breath and tasted it on his tongue that he shoved in her mouth. She tried her best to talk Kamal out of having sex. After all the throwing up she'd done she really wasn't in the mood. Turning her head to the side to avoid anymore of his sloppy kisses, Simone soon felt his street conditioned hands open up her blanket and rip her panties off.

"Please Kamal! I don't feel good!"

"Shut that shit up!" He replied using his body weight to cause her to fall back onto the couch. Kamal then dropped his pants exposing all nine and a half inches of his harden dick. Normally Simone enjoyed the thug like loving he'd put on her, but this time Kamal seemed to be vindictive and extra gangsta with it. "Who pussy is this?" He hissed growling in her ear. "This here belongs to me!"

Simone felt like an old rag doll as Kamal took his aggressions out on her body. He worked Simone off the couch and onto the floor where he really got rough. Blank expressions of nothingness filled her face with each movement of in and out thrusting violation Kamal gave to her. It didn't matter to Simone, she wasn't even there.

An unwilling participant, Simone day dreamed her self to a different world leaving Kamal to go for it and get his own nuts off, pants down to his ankles, Tim's still on.

Twenty long minutes of twisting Simone's hair between his fingers snatching back her head, one leg lifted over his shoulder, a purple unwanted passion mark on her neck and a carpet burn on her ass, Kamal finally was done screaming out in triumph as he climaxed.

"Damn! That was good!" He collapsed on Simone who didn't mutter a word. "Round two in a minute! But first go get ya mans some cold water!"

Simone got up going into the kitchen. Opening the refrigerator door the light inside shined on a butcher knife that was in the sink. *"I'm starting to hate his ass! I wish he was dead or at least back in prison."* Simone's mind kicked into overdrive as she imagined stabbing Kamal to death. *"Fuck that, I'm to pretty to be jailing it!"*

It would be hard, but for the time being her only choice was to deal with him. He was a damned good paymaster, but playing the game was getting old. Feeling the bottled water sweat in her hand gave her chills of deceit.

As she shut the door back she was startled by the sounds of *Slum Village* coming from behind the bags on the counter. "Oh shit! No he didn't leave that motherfucker!" Simone tried to grab a dish towel to muffle the ringtone blasting from Joey's cell phone. *"Out of all the times a bitch be trying to get a hold of his shit, now he decides to forget it!"*

Simone held the towel down covering the phone until it stopped ringing. But before she could get a chance to turn it off Kamal came into the kitchen fastening his pants.
"Where was that music coming from?"
"What music?"
"I thought I heard some damn music coming from somewhere."
"Maybe it was a car or something?" Simone had to get Kamal out of the kitchen quick. "Come on back in the living room so we can watch some videos."
"Naw I'm tight on all that! Now stop playing with me! I wanna know what the fuck was that I heard!"
"Boy, I don't know! You tripping!"
"Don't try to play me Simone! I ain't slow!"

Simone knew that Kamal was like a dog with a bone and wasn't gonna stop till he searched and found what he was looking for. She had to go into survival mode, unzip his pants and bring her famous A-Game to the table. *'When all else fails, drop down and suck a niggas dick!'*

Kamal was mesmerized and drifting in the zone. Simone was showing out sucking like her life depended on it and there was no tomorrow in sight. He'd forgotten all about the mystery music he'd just heard and was now totally preoccupied on the slurping sounds that a naked Simone was generating with her lips. Things were going perfect and blood thirsty Kamal was well on his way to cum for the second time and then hopefully to sleep, when once again wouldn't you know, *Slum Village* kicked in.

Simone stopped in mid slurp still down posted on her knees with a mouth full of dick looking up at crazed face Kamal as he leaned over moving the dish towel revealing the source of the noise…Joey's cell phone. Opening the strange phone showed the letters *'NFL'* flashing on the screen which everyone in Detroit, especially Kamal knew stood for *'NIGGAS FROM LINWOOD'*, his enemies.

Chapter Fourteen

"You know that feels soooo… good." Big Ace buried his face into the pillow letting Monique's hands rub and massage almost every inch of his huge body. After fifteen minutes of steaming hot shower water pouring down on him, he was feeling nice and this kingpin massage was like the icing on the cake to top the night off.

"Just close your eyes and let Monique take care of you."

"I hear you talking girl." Big Ace cooed like a baby. "Go ahead and handle your business."

Monique started at the back of his neck applying soft but firm squeezes. *"Oh yeah."* Then on to his strong shoulders where she paid extra special attention to. Using her palms she kneaded the still damp skin of his upper back. *"Oh shit, you good."* He let the words barely escape his lips as he drifted off. By the time Monique reached his lower torso with the touch of her magic hands, Big Ace was chilling in La-La Land, snoring his big ass off.

"Hey Baby." Monique whispered. "Are you asleep?"

Big Ace didn't open his mouth or even make any sort of motion to indicate he'd heard Monique's question.

"Hey Baby, did you hear me?" She posed the same question to him once again waiting to see what if anything he'd say. The only sound that she was met with was long drawn out snores.

"All that Big Willie talk and this mark buster sleep. Niggas kill me with all that bragging then punk out." Monique was on a mission but was still disappointed that she didn't get a chance to get some of that thick dick that Big Ace had between his legs. "I should cut the motherfucker off and take the bitch home for later!" Monique had to cover her mouth from laughing out loud at her own thoughts.

Slowly she reached over for her purse and retrieved her cell phone. The text message she was expecting was there. When she read it, the project bread female went into action. Carefully easing her body off the bed was a task because of all the weight she possessed. With every movement, Big Ace's snores took on a different tone. Monique wasn't sure if he'd wake up at any moment.

Successfully placing both feet on the floor Monique rose up instantly pausing as Big Ace lifted his head turning it to the other side. His clean shaven face was now facing her and appeared to be waking up. His eyes were wide open and seemed to be staring right at her and her every move. "Hey Baby." She tried seeing if she got a response but all he had to offer was a lot of gibberish. Monique stood there trembling decked out in her birthday suite trying to figure out what to do next. Big Ace was mumbling something about some dudes or a park and some guns. She frowned and sighed with relief when she realized that Big Ace was still fast asleep, but he was one of those weird sons of bitches that sleep with their eyes open. *"Ain't this some crazy shit?"*

Monique couldn't quite make out for certain what he was saying and taking into consideration that he was talking in his sleep she could give a fuck less. As long as Big Ace didn't catch her creeping towards the door throwing a monkey wrench in the game plan she'd be fine.

The sneaky conniving con artist tip-toed her naked body to the room door putting her fire engine red polished fingernails onto the chain sliding it off. Glancing back at Big Ace once more to ensure he wasn't awake yet, she then twisted the bolt unlocking the door.

"*Yes!*" She thought as she watched Big Ace appear to watch her walk around to the other side of the bed. Monique stopped momentarily looking at Big Ace's perfect muscular frame and licked her lips. "*Just stay asleep Boo Boo. I swear to God, It'd be such a waste to lullaby a motherfucker as fine as your black ass is.*"

She then disappeared into the bathroom leaving the door slightly cracked so she could hear clearly. Monique sat down on the toilet and played with herself with Big Ace in mind, to waste time as she waited for part three of her well crafted game plan to jump off.

Joey was on the freeway on his way to the hotel where Trevon was waiting. He reached under the seat getting his pistol sitting it on his lap as he drove. He tried to drive the speed limit knowing good and damn well that he was in Oakland County and out there the white man didn't play games with your ass. A Negro could easily get 90 days for coughing too loud in the middle of the night. With that in mind, Joey slowed down even more. It seemed as if it was destiny that kept causing them to cross paths with Kamal and his crew, so ten or fifteen minutes wouldn't matter that much.

Joey usually wasn't into all that gangbang madness, but he felt he had no choice this go around. It's one thing to blow a lot of smoke out ya mouth with idle threats, but it's a different ball game on a whole different level when a nigga starts actually busting. That's when and where true players draw the line and chaos kicks in.

While gripping the steering wheel, trying his best to seem inconspicuous to the State Boys, Joey thought about Simone and how strange and jumpy she was acting. As long as he'd known her, she never ever would let him get out of her sight without getting some dough, especially some that he'd already promised her. Until he finished with the business at hand, Simone would have to be on the back burner. But that still didn't stop him from thinking. "This the second time tonight she done let me slide on the money tip. I wonder what her slick ass is up to now?

Monique removed her hand from between her legs and peeked out the door. She took a deep breath as the knob slowly turned. The sounds of Big Ace's snores filled the room as the three masked men crept inside with their guns pointed directly at the bed. The first man to enter was immediately thrown off by the fact that Big Ace was lying in the bed looking dead at them without say a single solitary word.

"What the fuck!" The man yelled.

Big Ace blinked his eyes twice and squinted trying to get a grip of what was happening. Before he could get a chance to mutter a word the second guy rushed over slamming the side of his gun into the side of his head. The force of the blow caused a gash to open wide and blood to flow down the side of Big Ace's face.

With the third man shutting the door, the real reason for the invasion became apparent as Big Ace was beat almost unconscious. He was gangsta to the tenth degree as he took punch after punch without so much as one word of protest. After being stumped several good old fashion times and then kicked twice in the mouth, Big Ace watched helplessly as one of the mask men ran in the bathroom where Monique pretended to be hiding at and snatched her out. Her nude body was hard to cover as she screamed trying to act as if she was fighting off the robbers. After a brief struggle, the masked man backhanded her once hard and covered her mouth with his hand. With the other hand he probed every inch of her nude body while she let the fake tears flow. Feeling on her huge breast, then sticking his fingers one by one inside her already wet pussy, she tried to yank away and resist.

"Bring the tramp over here so her man can see her." One of the men ordered.

"Lay her big butt on the floor near this sucker!" The next said pushing a hysterical Monique to the ground.

"Please don't! Please!" She sobbed and pleaded.

Monique was good at this part of the routine, this was her specialty. She always had to make things look good, because if she didn't one of her many victims might get suspicious to the set up scam, catch her fat ass on the streets and kill the bitch. So the game continued and after twenty long dragged out minutes of Big Ace being forced to watch all three mask men taking turns having sex with Monique, even violating her anally he saw each spit in her face leaving her, unbeknownst to him, nymphomaniac ass balled up in a corner happy about the different dicks that just were inside of her.

"*Damn that was the shit.*" She thought to herself.

Big Ace was now face down naked on the dirty carpet, with a drenched combination of blood and perspiration dripping off of him. As bad as he wanted to come to the females' rescue and his own he had three guns pointed directly at him and his hands duct taped behind his bruised back. The street warrior couldn't do anything but wait and see what else the gunmen had in store.

In the midst of him injured and suffering he tried his best to at least recognize the voices that were coming from behind the mask but couldn't. Laying there in a growing pool of blood, Big Ace thought back to the shoot out at the park and came to the conclusion that this whole fucked up situation must be somehow connected. "*If I get out of this alive, them motherfuckers gonna pay!*"

"Should we let this punk live or what?"

"Naw, let's do his ass!"

"Yeah, let's kill both they asses!"

After a short discussion that was already preplanned the three intruders went through Big Ace's pockets taking all his money, his wallet, jewelry and Monique's purse. The trio neared the door and turned around to double check making sure they hadn't left anything.

The first two were outside the room as the third reached on the floor by the bed and grabbed the last take for the night before making his exit. "Thanks Player, good looking out! I need a new pair of these!"

Big Ace and Monique watched the dude deliver the final kick in the balls for the night by taking the brand new fresh pair of Tim's that Big Ace had just bought earlier. With the couple now alone, both bloody and sore, a still naked Monique was relentless in playing the scenario all the way out. Her whimpers of pain were of soap opera category. The way she crawled over to Big Ace's body wrapping her arms around him was sheer genius. Hands shaking with fear as she tore the duct tape off.

Monique might have been born and raised in Detroit's grimiest projects. A hundred or so pounds over weight, different baby daddies, a head full of weave and couldn't dress like shit. Sure the tramp had the unsophisticated grace of a wild Lama in heat and the educational level of a kindergartener, but there wasn't a person that walked the face of the earth or moon that could deny the chick could act her ass off.

"Oh my God Baby! Are you okay?" She closely held a dazed Big Ace.

"Naw, I think you better get some help." He managed to say. "Call my boy Kamal. Tell him them dudes from the park must've followed us or something."

Monique knew calling Kamal would be a bad idea. Even though Big Ace didn't suspect her involvement in the robbery, her crew needed time to get out of dodge and back safely across town. Instead the actress stalled for time by pulling the phone down off the nightstand by its cord and slowly dragging it over towards her. With a deep breath of desperation Monique dialed the operator.

"Hello front desk…We need an ambulance in room 117!"

Chapter Fifteen

Trevon watched as the men one by one entered room 117. His adrenalin was rising as his heart rate increased. It was eating him up inside with every passing moment that he focused his mind on the goings on behind the closed door. *"Damn, what the fuck is they doing in that bitch?"* Paying attention to the burgundy curtains just in case they moved revealing a quick peek or maybe hearing a gunshot or two was all that Trevon was waiting for.

   A couple of cars turned into the lot parking in front of their rooms. Happy couples walking hand and hand who had no idea what was probably going on in the room right next to theirs, laughed and joked. Those few late night stragglers reminded a hawk eyed Trevon to try once again to get in touch with Joey to warn him.

   Glancing downwards long enough to see the redial button and push it, he listened to four long rings.

"Pick up Nigga! Come on pick up!" On the fifth ring as soon as he was about to hang up a strange voice answered. "YEAH... WHO THIS!!!!????"

"Hello." Trevon paused with uncertainty not recognizing the voice on the other end of the line.

"I said who this?" Kamal demanded once more.

Trevon took his eyes off room 117 so he could check to make sure that he'd pushed the right button. When he read Joey's number out one by one to himself he knew that something was wrong. "Man who the fuck is this playing on my people's phone?"

Kamal shook his head at a tearful Simone as he yelled into the cell phone at the caller. "Bitch ass nigga! Don't be getting loud with me! I'm the one asking the questions. Now like I said, who the fuck is this?"

Trevon pushed end, hanging up on the mystery man believing that Nextel must've been slipping and got its wires crossed. "Let me do this dumb shit again." As he took his time scrolling down his list of contacts he came to Joey's name and hit call.

Simone tried to get up and run out of the kitchen, but was stopped by Kamal's huge hands snatching her back. "Who's God damn shit is this?" Kamal wrapped his hand firmly around her hair twisting it until his knuckles were pressed into her scalp. "And matter of fact, fuck that! Why you got one of them Linwood Niggas calling this motherfucker?"

"Wait Kamal!"

"Wait for what bitch?" He tossed the phone back on the counter. "What lie you about to tell me?"

Simone had to come up with something quick. "I'm trying to tell you if you just give me a chance."

Smack... "There goes your chance hoe! Now answer me!"

"That must be Prayer's phone. She must've left it when she was fixing my food."

Smack, Smack... "Don't lie to me Simone!"

"I'm not, I swear on Lil T's life that's Prayer's phone!"

"Don't make me sock you!" He stiffened his grip.

"Please Kamal, you're hurting me."

"Like that shit matter any to me!"

With her face beet red and an imprint of Kamal's hand plastered across it, Simone started to hyperventilate from fear. She'd seen Kamal pissed off before, having had plenty of ass kickings administered by him, but this time was different. He had the un-denying cold callous persona of a psychotic killer on a late night horror movie.

Before Simone could concoct a way to weasel her way out of what could easily turn out to be the worst beating she ever experienced, Kamal struck her twice more in her face, only this time with a closed fist. One blow grazed her jaw, while the other found its way to her ear. As he let go of her hair, Simone flew into the side of the stainless steel refrigerator seeing stars as she made contact.

Kamal cracked his knuckles walking over to an already wounded Simone with more brutal thoughts in store as she was trying her best to regain her senses. Dazed and confused by the hit she'd just taken, his son's mother was too weak to move. Just as he raised his boot to stump her, *Slum Village,* distracted him.

"Oh, I see your punk ass boyfriend is calling back!" Simone had no comment remaining quiet as a mouse as

Kamal went over to the counter once again answering Joey's ringing cell phone. "*NFL*, yeah that's his hoe ass!" He grunted pushing talk. "YEAH NIGGA! Why you keep calling my motherfucking girl?"

Trevon was speechless in responding to who ever had his boys' phone. Less than a half a hour ago, Joey was just talking on the shit and now this clown had it. He had a bad feeling about the whole thing, knowing that it couldn't be anything nice behind it.

"Listen Playa! Where dude at whos phone you holding?"
"And what dude is that?"
"Come on Player and stop bullshittin'. You know who cell you got! NFL NIGGA!"

Kamal slammed his hand on a loaf of bread squeezing it with anger screaming across the kitchen. "Damn Simone, I thought this was that hoe Prayer's phone!"
"I..I..I..thought.." She tried to speak but couldn't get the words out without stuttering.
"Man, shut the fuck up!" Kamal threw the smashed loaf at her head.

Trevon heard him say Simone's name and shit started to click. This had to be one of her trick busters that done got a hold of Joey's phone. "Put Simone on!"

"She busy about to get an ass kicking!" Kamal fired back.

"Oh yeah? Well that's between you and her. All I wanna know is where is my peoples at?"

"Dig dis Linwood! Ya some hoe ass motherfuckers and next time I see anyone of yall it's on!"

"You coward bitch!" Trevon snickered smugly. "Whoever this is, you don't want none!" As he and the dude exchanged insults and promises, Trevon wondered exactly who this buster was.

"Whatever Guy! Just tell your peoples to stay the fuck away from my pussy!"

Kamal got a glimpse of Simone trying to crawl out the kitchen unnoticed and snapped. "Did I tell your bitch ass to move?"

"I think I hear Lil T crying." She whined breathing hard.

"So what?"

"He needs me!"

"So fucking what Simone!"

"But…"

"But what? I told you not the hell to move Simone, now I'm not fucking around wit ya ass no more. If you even blink an eye, I'm beating ya ass and Lil T! Now try me!"

"Please don't!" Simone begged sounding sincere.

"I warned you bitch, now I'm about to show you!"

Trevon knew that Simone deserved and needed to get mashed for playing both ends against the middle and getting caught up, but this fool was talking about putting his hands on Joey's son.

"Damn Dude! Why you threatening a kid? Yous a hoe!"

"Stay outta my business!" Kamal ended his conversation with Trevon by major league pitching the cell phone into Simone's leg causing an almost immediate dark red bruise to form on her light skin matching the ones on her face.

Trevon tried calling back but got the voice mail. *"Damn Joey. Where you at?"*

He looked back out the hotel room window anxious for his boys arrival, just in time to witness the three mask gunman exit room 117 just as quiet as they had entered, commotion free. Five minutes later he heard police sirens.

OUT 4 $ELF

☼

Joey was a few minutes away from touching bases with Trevon when a gang of cop cars roared by. Their obvious unmistakably white suburban asses had their hats on tight and their guns polished ready to burn a nigga down.

Joey held his breath as each one passed him not even looking in his direction. "Whew, that was close." He cut his eyes over at his gun which was still riding shotgun. When he turned onto Dequindre, he was faced with the police vehicles again. They were swarming in and around the entire perimeter of the hotel where Trevon was at. *"What this fool done did? I told his ass to chill!"*

Turning into a nearby gas station so he could get his thoughts together and call Trevon, Joey searched the car for his cell phone when he realized that he'd left it back at Simone's house on the kitchen counter. *"Shit, I know her jealous ass calling every number on that motherfucker!"*

Luckily for Joey, he was in the White Mans Territory and it was a payphone conveniently located on the far side of the gas station. He walked over and lifted up the receiver and actually heard a dial tone. Back in the hood, a Negro could search until the soles of his Tim's wore out and still couldn't find a payphone, at least one that worked. Depositing the correct amount of change the recorded voiced requested, Joey dialed Trevon's cell.

"Hey Dude! What up?"

"Damn Joey! Boost Mobile! Where the fuck your ass at?"

"I'm down at the corner. I seen a bunch of them boys and thought your ass did something drastic."

"Naw, I didn't have to!" Trevon rushed through his explanation. "Some other Cats with Halloween mask on creeped they asses. I'm still in my room chilling."

"Damn, they straight holding you hostage huh?"

"Joey Man, later for all that. I just called your cell phone and.."

"I know I left that bad boy back at Simone's. What she doing…answering the motherfucker or what?" Joey laughed at his son's Moms.

"Naw Guy! Some lame wanna be gangsta answered that bitch!"

"What!"

"Yeah nigga. Just now!"

"Alright then Tre, is you tight? I'm about to go catch this bitch in the act!"

"I'm tight Dogg, do you! And chin check that buster for me! It's one thing to slap around a Trick, but I heard that fool talking about whopping up on your seed!"

"Lil T?"

"Yeah Dude! That's what he said while he was smacking ole girl around."

"You bullshittin'?"

"Naw Cuz, I heard her screaming! Ain't no telling what that buster over there doing right about now!"

"I'm out! I'll holler!"

Joey slammed the receiver down jumping back in his car and headed back to Simone's. Fuck the police! Fuck the speed limit! And Fuck any stray ass sissy fool that thought he could get away with putting they hands on his son! He loved Lil T! That was his little man and he'd walk threw a blazing hot barn fire with gasoline underwear for him. So any motherfucker putting they hands on him was out of the question.

Chapter Sixteen

"It's now a little after four o'clock in the morning in Detroit and you're listening to 105.9FM. The temperature is a balmy 75 degrees which is unusual for this time of year. You've got ya main man, DJ Smooth-N-Groove waking some of you early shift factory workers up so you can punch that clock and helping those late night party hopping, casino going, can't seemed to go to sleep folks chill out. Whatever applies to you, grab a hold Motown and reminisced on a little bit of this..."

Chari was in her bed with the darkness surrounding her. She was lonely with no one to keep her company except the sounds of the radio. The rhythmic beat of the song caused her to re-examine her life. *"Damn, I'm tired of living alone. I wish I had someone to love me like Drake loves Prayer or even that love Simone's crazy self gets."* It was at that very moment in time, Chari decided that as soon as she got off from work and got home, she was gonna stop fronting and ask Trevon over to dinner.

Who knows, maybe he was her knight in shinning armor. It was worth taking the chance and giving it a shot if it meant love. Chari knew that if it was one guy on the entire earth that had no designs on trying to get with her friend, Simone, it was Trevon. And with Simone the feeling was mutual.

Prayer stayed on the telephone with Drake as he drove down the Interstate heading back from Baltimore. The couple was ecstatic that he'd concluded all his business dealings early and would be home shortly after daybreak. Listening to her radio in the background took the pair on a heartfelt trip down memory lane to the time that they were young teenagers.

Taking the bus downtown to Hart Plaza for the summer festivals, walking hand and hand at Northland, going skating at Wheels and even their first real kiss on the side of Drake's Grandmother's house on Glendale were the main topics of the night. After all the turmoil and dangerous crap Simone had taken her and Chari through at the club, Prayer was more than ready for Drake to enroll back in school to finish getting his degree and leave the Game alone all together. He was already headed that direction, but she intended on giving him that extra nudge she felt he needed.

Trevon watched out the hotel window as the ambulance drivers rolled their gurney out with a body on it. After careful inspection from a far, Trevon realized that it was Big Ace. They had an oxygen mask over his face and were moving at a fast rate of speed. The female, that he recognized as, Monique was following closely behind with a blanket wrapped around her. The police seemed to be taking notes as crime scène cameras started to flash.

Everyone from the Hotel Managers, the guest and nosey passersby's wanted to see what crime had taken place. Even when the ambulance pulled off in route to the local hospital, the crowd still stayed gossiping as the police investigated trying to make heads or tails about the true story, since Monique was acting like she was in shock.

Trevon was trapped inside his room and laid across the bed with only his gun to keep him company.

He turned the radio on his favorite station to pass the time away as he waited for Joey to call him and fill him in on how he ended up beating the piss out of the big mouthed wanksta who answered the phone and Simone's no good behind.

Yvette's headphones were turned up to the highest volume. She had grown accustom to sleeping like that every night to avoid hearing the thunderous like sounds of Ms. Holmes snores. It was four o'clock in the morning and she still couldn't sleep. With the combination of Simone smacking her foster mother, who in turn called the authorities and the thought of Simone totally cutting her off, which meant no more cute outfits or purses, Yvette was up and down all night.

Watching the stars twinkle and the bright full moon shine over the row of vacant houses near the corner, the young girl couldn't help but notice all the after hour traffic that was opening and closing doors over at Simone's house. Even though Simone often had company, this much in and out was not ordinary.

As Yvette bopped her head from side to side to the old school jams that DJ Smooth-N-Groove was playing, she first saw Joey come over carrying some bags. *"He's so nice. He's always bringing Simone or Lil T something."* A little bit after that and four songs later, she observed Joey running off the porch with his feet barely touching the stairs, jumping in his car and racing off down the block. *"Where's he going so fast? He just got there!"*

Before the commercial about the *Summer Jam Concert* and the after party at *The Marroitt* on E. Jefferson could go off and the music start back playing, Yvette saw Kamal pull up in the driveway behind Simone's Lexus and bang on her front door. *"Dang gee Simone! That was close!"*

With contempt for Kamal in her heart for the way she'd witness him talk to her idol, Simone, not to mention the way he mistreated Lil T, Yvette turned her lip up with disgust as she watched him pee in the grass. *"Ughh…He so nasty! I hate him!"*

When Simone finally opened the door and Yvette saw him push his way in the house, she laid back down in her bed and tried to get some rest. *"Hey this my song!"*

Chapter Seventeen

☼

"Simone, I'm not fucking around with ya bitch ass no more!" Kamal used her ears as handles grabbing her up off the floor throwing her into the living room.

"I'm sorry! I'm sorry!" Simone gasped for air as Kamal harshly stomped his Tim down in her stomach. "Please I can't breathe!"

Simone turning pale as a ghost was not a deterrent for Kamal as he applied more pressure. Simone's once beautiful eyes were now bloodshot and rolling towards the back of her throbbing head. With snot and mucus filling her face she was well on her way to pass completely out.

"Tramp it ain't that easy!" Kamal removed his boot backhanding her twice to bring her out of it. "Now get the fuck up and take this ass whopping like a woman!"

She shook glaring at him with disbelief as he got her back up to feet only to give a massive body blow to her side causing her to crumble once more falling on the carpet.

"You wanna lie and creep around behind a Niggas' back and shit!" Kamal spit a huge glob down on her. "I be out here putting my motherfucking freedom on the line for your slut ass and you giving away my pussy to the next Cat!"

Simone's cracked dry lips quivered as she tried unsuccessfully to speak.

"Don't even try it Simone! All them games you be playing is the hell over! Where is my fucking car keys?" He fumed with anger. "You ain't about to be driving no other man around in the Lexus I got you pushing!"

When Kamal saw no movement or reaction, he realized that his son's mother was now unconscious. That was his cue as he went through out Simone's house like Hurricane Katrina destroying everything he came in contact with. He ripped the fabric off her new furniture, cut the cord on her flat screen television before snatching it down off the wall mount and smashing every DVD he could lay his hands on. Whether he purchased the items for Simone or not didn't matter to him as he caused non- repairable damage to her property.

In the midst of the noise and commotion he was making, Kamal heard sounds coming from the hallway and turned around to see his son, Lil T, emerge out the darkness crying for his mother.

"Go back to bed!" He ordered.

"Mommy...Mommy..." Lil T whined with a constant flow of tears streaming while wiping his eyes. "Mommy..."

"Shut the fuck up with all that sissy shit and take your ass back to bed!"

"I want my Mommy...Mommy...Mommy..."

"What the fuck did I just say?" Kamal approached the tiny innocent little boy. "Get the fuck on!"

The loud tone of Kamal's voice only made matters worse as a scared Lil T began to sob more. He held his hands up toward Kamal to pick him up and take him to his Mommy like he'd done in the past, but got no response but fury as one of the men he was taught to call *'Da-Da'* knocked his arms down to his side. Kamal cupped the small child's head in his hands turning him around shoving him towards bedroom. Lil T was thrown off balance and confused as to what was taking place.

"Go get in that bed! Now! Before I beat your little crybaby Momma Boy's ass!" Kamal yanked Lil T's arm damn near out of the socket as he tossed him into his room and onto the bed yelling out one more final demand before closing the door tightly shut in his face. "Stay the fuck in here and lay the hell down!"

As Kamal returned to the living room to finish his tirade of physical assault on Simone, he could still hear their son's piercing screams. *"What the fuck?"* With his eyes darting from the space on the carpet where he'd left Simone laying to every corner of the room, Kamal searched for where she'd disappeared to. *"Oh, this bitch think I'm playing with her ass."*

Not saying a word, he went over to the front door putting the double lock on. Then he went into the kitchen to slide the chain on the back entrance.

"Alright whore. You only making the beat down worse when I find that ass!" Kamal knew Simone was hiding somewhere in the front of the house because it was no way she could've snuck by him in the back. "You only pissing me off more and more you slut bag dick sucking tramp!"

After a quick check behind the couch and love seat, he spotted a foot sticking from under the dinning room table. Kamal took his time heading in that direction making Simone sweat it out. "Do you really think I'm gonna let you get away with playing me for a sucker? Especially with one of them Linwood motherfuckers?" He grinned wickedly running his tongue across his teeth. "You got the game and me all fucked up!"

Simone's hearted pounded with fear as she watched the soles of Kamal's boots submerge into the thick padded carpet and closer to her. *"Damn, I messed up for real this time."* Her life seemed to flash before her eyes as one of her son's fathers dug his strong fingers into her ankle and tried dragging her out into the open.

"Stop! Stop!" She kicked at him in an attempt to break loose. "I ain't do shit! I swear! I ain't do shit!"

"Shut up bitch!"

"Please Kamal!"

"Hell naw!"

"Let me go! Pleeeez….."

"Fuck you Simone! I ain't done with your ass yet!"

For what seemed like an eternity, the two of them struggled back and forth. Simone was already injured and at a disadvantage by being a woman. She was exhausted, not being able to fight and hold him off any longer. Her body gave out going completely limp as he climbed on top of her.

"You two timing project rat!" His fist came down by her face into the carpet. "You can't beat a grown ass man!"

Simone panted repeatedly trying to catch her breath as Kamal pressed his sweaty body down smothering hers. She couldn't move one inch as they were now nose to nose. Kamal was furious as he continued to talk shit.

"Your ass wanna give the pussy away?" He momentary waited knowing that he wouldn't get an answer. "Well after tonight that crap faggot nigga can have your tainted broke ass!" Kamal reached one hand up to his mouth removing his fronts. He saw look of panic on Simone's face as he rammed the gold curved mouth ornament deep inside of her pussy. Simone was speechless as Kamal's continuous heinous movements tried to ruin her for life. "Please don't." She muttered in distress.

"Now let's see you give this worthless stankin' motherfucker away!" Kamal laughed.

Simone's arms were stretched out and lying above her head. The strong traumatic scraping force that Kamal was applying pushed her fingertips close to a small plastic crate that she kept cleaning supply's in. With her skin numb and tingling from the misery of the torture she was enduring, Simone grabbed a bottle of Windex Glass Cleaner and squirted the preoccupied crazed Kamal in his eyes causing an almost immediate halt to his unthinkable act.

"Get off me!" Screaming at the top of her lungs Simone managed to squirm away and crawl to the other room.

"Alright bitch! You gonna die for that!" Kamal got off the floor blinded by the chemicals in both eyes and felt his way to the kitchen sink. "I'm gonna kill you!"

As he stumbled passing by a still naked Simone, she smashed a hand carved imported vase across the back of his head. A candy apple colored thick moisture of blood started to ooze through his perfectly parted braids and drip down. Simone paused, waiting to see if he would fall.

He slowly reached up touching the open gash and got a handful of wetness. Kamal was dazed but still on his feet in search of water to rinse and relieve the burning sensation in his stinging eyes.

Now was Simone's time to make a get away. Running to the front door and unlocking it in an attempt to escape, she looked down realizing that she didn't have any clothes on. *"Oh My God! Oh My God!"* She pondered as she heard the water in the kitchen running. *"What I'm gonna do now? Oh shit! Oh shit!"* Simone snatched her cell phone off the table and ran towards the bathroom to lock her self in and call for help. She was less than ten feet away from the door when she heard Lil T calling out for her from the hallway.

"Mommy! Mommy!" He whined getting closer.

Simone saw her small son on the other side of the living room coming towards her. Out the corner of her eye she saw an infuriated Kamal also heading in her direction. *"Oh shit! Damn!"* She thought as she made the selfish decision to leave her baby to fin for him self on the other side of the bathroom door. Turning the lock leaning her weary body against the thin wooden door, Simone pushed 911 on her cell twice before realizing that the battery was completely dead.

Bam, Bam, Bam…Kamal's fist hit the door causing the frame to shake. *Bam, Bam, Bam.* His boots were now kicking the splitting wood. Time was ticking!

Joey raced down the freeway with one thought in mind, Lil T. He loved his woman, but she was a big girl and could take care of her self. The anticipation of getting to Simone's house to find out what in the hell was taking place made the veins in Joey's neck bulge. If his small son needed him, he was gonna be there even if it meant breaking every law that the State of Michigan had on its books.

"*Damn, this traffic is crazy for this time of night. Where all these motherfuckers going?*" He swerved around a huge semi-truck and pushed the gas pedal close to the floor. Flying by an old school Monte Carlo and one broke down Checker Cab, Joey made good time. Less than ten minutes later he saw his exit in sight. "*Linwood Ave.- ¼ Mile.*"

Joey took the same exact path that only a short time earlier Kamal had taken. Flying around the deep curve pass *Fenkell,* he never let up on the speed. *Oakman Blvd., Davison Ave.,* and finally *Glendale St.* where the red light and crossing traffic stopped him. *"Ahh…Shit!"*

His first mind told him to fuck all the cars and make his move, but seeing a car load of *'Detroit's Finest'* harassing some late night creepers shut that idea down. After all, he did have his gun sitting right on the seat next to him in full plain view. When the light turned green, he slowly drove the speed limit pass the police glancing back in his rear mirror to make sure they weren't on him.

"Five more blocks to Simone's." Joey tapped on the steering wheel with his palms sweating.

"Get out my house, before I call the police!" Simone tried bluffing the already agitated Kamal.

"Call the sons of bitches!" He kicked once more. "By the time they slow asses get here the only thing they gonna find is your dead body!"

"I'm not playing!" She screamed through the close door.

"I ain't either bitch!"

In the midst of their back and forth threats, Lil T's cries were louder and much more heart wrenching. He was now right underfoot of Kamal who only had one thing on his devious agenda at this point, vengeance. The sounds of Lil T's voice were like a powerful echo to Simone who felt she had no choice but to try to remain barricaded. "You better come out here and get this little motherfucker before I kick his ass up on the mantle." Kamal collared his son up shaking him wildly.

"Mommy!...I want my Mommy!" Lil T begged snotty nosed, face full of tears.

"You listening to this soft faggot?" Kamal used Lil T's tiny framed body ramming it against the door for Simone to hear. "He wants you bitch!"

Lil T whimpered with pain as he was being used as a pawn in his parents' tragic game.

"Please stop Kamal, please! What in the hell is wrong with you?" Simone was trembling from fear as she searched the bathroom with her eyes for any sort of a weapon. "How can you do that bullshit to your own child?!"

"I'm counting to three hoe and if you don't come out I'm gonna give his little ass another taste of the beat down you got coming!" He warned.

"Don't Kamal!"

"One…"

"I swear I'm gonna call the police!"

"Two…"

"Please! Please! Don't hurt my baby!"

"Three…"

"Wait! Wait! Wait! I'm begging you!"

"Hell naw! Fuck you and him!"

As if on cue, a stone faced Kamal grabbed a defenseless Lil T by his long braids, his own son, his own supposed to be flesh and blood and swung him around twice then finally let go flinging his wilted body across the living room resulting in him crashing into the wall. *"BAM!"* Lil T appeared lifeless as he lay near the front door beside the couch with a small trickle of blood coming out the corner of his mouth. Kamal wasted no time as he got his gun and put one up top. "Okay Simone! You up next Trick!" He turned the radio on loud to muffle the sounds of his plans.

With complete momentary utter silence in the house, Simone knew that her first born was hurt and now it was really life or death. As all of sudden sounds of Rap filled the air, she leaped to her feet opening up the medicine cabinet pulling out a straight razor. "I'm gonna kill him!"

Joey turned the corner out of view of the police and flew down Simone's block. When he got in front of her house he slammed on his breaks, threw the car in park and jumped out gun in hand. *"What the fuck is this bullshit about?"* He couldn't believe that the same F-150 from earlier was all up in his Baby Momma's driveway. *"I know this coward ain't in there with my family!"* He placed his hand on the hood to see if it was still warm, but it wasn't. That let him know that *'Mr. Shoot Up The Park In Broad Daylight'* had been there for some time. *"Damn! I just left this motherfucker! That bitch work quick!"* Joey cautiously walked up on the porch. Within five seconds of standing there, he heard Lil T cry, a thud, silence then loud music. The loyal father wasted no time kicking the door almost off the hinges confronting the unknown.

Chapter Eighteen

"What the fuck?" Kamal turned facing the door as the loud noise and vibration shook the entire house.

"Oh hell naw!" As soon as it flew, open Joey immediately spotted Lil T lying on the floor spread eagle facing the ceiling. "What the fuck your ass do to my motherfucking son?" He revengefully wasted no time in waiting for his response opening fire on a shocked Kamal who distinctly dove behind a chair taking cover.

Letting off round after round, Joey was sure that he'd hit Kamal at least once or twice in the lower body. *"Who the fuck is this punk?"* Joey thought while never letting up on the trigger. *"And where the hell is Simone?"* He could only hope and pray at this point that her fate wasn't as worst as Lil T's appeared to be. *"And how the fuck he know her sneaky ass?"* That Scooby Doo Mystery only added more heat to his already boiling adrenaline.

"Shit! I think I'm hit!" Kamal looked down to his hip realizing that he had a gaping tear in his pants and darken blood starting to soak through. "And what that Nigga mean his son?" If he lived past daylight, he would have to deal with that bullshit then, but for now, ole boy was on a crucial straight high alert solider detail. Kamal was 100% true to the game and the streets that helped raised him. He indeed had caught a few hot ones, but had no worldly intentions of going out like a pussy. He lifted up, all Scarface style and shit, returning fire ripping Joey a nice size hole in his left shoulder as well as his chest. "NOW WHAT MOTHERFUCKER?" Kamal hissed with anger. "NOW WHAT?"

"NFL NIGGA! WE DON'T DIE WE MULTIPLY!" Joey shouted back as he let off one more round into a demented Kamal before dropping to the ground near Lil T's still motionless tiny body.

"FUCK LINWOOD!" Kamal howled as a boiling hot sensation torn through his upper groin area then raced to his stomach throwing him back against a bookshelf knocking the loud stereo and its speakers to the ground.

"NAW FUCK YOU!" Joey managed to get out as he turned his head towards his young son and reached out for his small hand.

Both of Lil T's potential fathers were severely wounded. At this point, it was uncertain as to who'd gotten the best of the other as they both bled and moaned.

Simone was still in the bathroom straight razor in hand, but was smart enough to lie down in the bathtub to shield her self from a stray bullet. *"Please God let my son be okay. I swear I'm done playing games."* She prayed as the sound of a door getting kicked not to mention the rapid gunshots gave her chills. Jumping with every passing echo she shivered. *"Damn, what the fuck is happening? What is his crazy ass out there doing?"*

She'd no idea that Joey doubled back to save the day so to speak and was now in her living room taking part in destroying her already twisted world. Simone was under the impression that a jealous immature Kamal was just showing his natural black ass, shooting holes in her furniture and walls to teach her a lesson.

He'd torn up her house on several prior occasions before when shit didn't go his way, spattering bleach on half of her wardrobe including two full length fur coats, pissing in and on every shoe in her closet and worst of all when the satanic asshole killed Lil T's puppy by snapping his neck, so nothing Simone thought Kamal was doing tonight surprised her one bit. She just hoped her son was safe.

After another big deafening sound, Simone carefully peeked her head up from the tub. Two long grueling minutes drug by before she made the hesitant decision to go back to the door and listen for any movement. She hoped that Kamal had finally given in, done enough damage and left.

"It's quiet out there." It was the loudest silence she'd ever heard as she whispered to her self feeling on the light tan ivory handle of the razor. "I need to go check on my son and stop thinking about myself."

It was as if someone up above clicked on the light switch in Simone's head informing her that she wasn't only responsible for her own well being, but also Lil T's. She wrapped a fluffy white bath towel around her naked body and took a deep breath. As the frightened mother gradually turned the lock cracking the bathroom door just slightly enough to see, Simone smelled the strange mixture of gun powder and blood. Stepping out a few short feet she saw the bottom of Kamal's boots and heard him sigh in pain.

"What the fuck is he trying to pull? And where is my motherfucking son?"

Yvette leaped from her bed running to the window. The sound of Joey's screeching tires could more than likely be heard blocks over. As she watched him rush, gun in hand, over to Kamal's F-150 that was parked in the driveway and touch the hood, she knew that her hero and mentor, Simone was seconds away from being busted. *"Damn!"*

Joey was at the door a few seconds before all of a sudden Yvette saw him kick the son of a bitch in and loud crazy gunshots jump off. *"Oh my God!"* She panicked as she flew out of her room grabbing the telephone calling 911. Ms. Holmes as well as the entire neighborhood made their way onto their front porches to see the outcome.

Chapter Nineteen

Thinking that Kamal was running game on her, Simone took her time in approaching him as she infuriately saw the condition of her once perfect home. *"Look at my front door! He gonna die for this crap! I'm just gonna be with Joey from now on out! Period!"*

Simone got close and couldn't believe her eyes. There was big bad Kamal, lying helpless on her new carpet semi-conscious, drenched in blood moaning for help. *"What the hell! This shit is crazy as a fuck!?"* She was confused.

Before she could process what had really taken place she turned her head hearing another noise of agony and came face to face with her worst nightmare yet. Joey was stretched out near the front door gasping for air as he coughed up dark globs of blood. There to his right side also sprawled stationary, Simone was horrified to see Lil T, her only child. *"Oh My God! Oh no! Oh my God!"*

Forgetting all about Kamal, a towel clad Simone ran to her son and Joey. One look at her other Babies Daddy made her feel instant queasiness and sick to her stomach. She then focused her attention on Lil T, dropping the razor from her hand and leaning protectively over her child's body rubbing his cheeks asking him repeatedly if he was all right and if he could hear her.

"Mommy loves you Baby!" She reassured him as her maternal instinct kicked in. "Are you okay? Talk to me!"

"Yes Mommy." Lil T finally cried out a soft reply.

"Don't worry baby. Mommy's gonna get help!" She was getting up to call 911 when she was stopped.

"Simone." Joey some how managed to lift his arm out towards her still coughing up blood. "Is my son okay? Are you okay?" He had a massive hole in his chest big enough for Simone to stick her fist in. His shirt was soaked in perspiration as his stomach raced up and down. "I'm sorry it took me so long to get here." Joey struggled with every word he spoke. "I let you and my son down." The devoted father's breathing was getting more faint and raspy with each second that ticked by. "I tried, I tried."

"No you didn't let us down Joey!" Simone confessed hysterically in tears. "This is all my fault! I'm so sorry Sweetheart! I'm so sorry!" Relentlessly pleading while realizing that her constant knight in shinning armor was slipping away from her, she shouldered the blame. "If it wasn't for me and all my scheming, shit would've been so different for us. Can you forgive me Joey?"

Simone, not caring about the awful state that he was in, pressed her face closed to his and apologized one last time. "I'm so sorry! I'm gonna call 911. Just hold on Baby!" She wanted to own up about all the awful games she'd been playing with him, Kamal and Lil T, but knew at this point the shit really didn't matter. The only thing that truly mattered was him getting medical attention.

Joey didn't answer, so Simone raised her head to look in his eyes in an attempt to beg for forgiveness once again. A weary Joey seemed to be staring straight through Simone as he started shaking violently going into convulsions. Within a brief snap of the fingers the young man, who was a son, a possible father and a loyal friend to the bitter end, Mr. Joey Ladon Carter, born March 17, 1981, was gone.

☼

Frantically in denial about the events that were quickly unfolding, Simone was still praying to God that this was just one of her terrible nightmares. Some old Twilight Zone bullshit! It had to be! Maybe she drank too much at the club and was hallucinating.

"This ain't happening! *This shit ain't happening*!" She insistently mumbled holding Joey's bullet riddled body rocking him in her arms like a newborn. *"Joey is still alive! I'm only dreaming! I'm gonna wake up at any time!"*

Off in the distance, Simone heard police sirens that brought her back to reality as she laid Joey gently down. "I'm sorry Joey." She kissed his lips in spite of all the blood and mucous. "Even though I always knew deep down inside that Lil T wasn't yours, I was still out 4 self."

The once pure white towel she was wearing was now completely soiled saturated with his blood along with hers from the beating and brutal rape she'd suffered at the hands of Kamal. With the sirens getting closer, she knew she had enough of Kamal. More than the average person could take. He stood for everything evil in her life.

In Simone's now deranged, mind Joey was gone because of him and not the deadly game of Baby Daddy Russian Roulette she was playing every second since Lil T's first conception. Coldly picking her straight razor off the floor Simone walked towards a still suffering Kamal. The man she was certain was truly her son's no good Daddy. As her bruised battered body got closer and the sirens got louder her palms began to sweat.

"Get over here and help me trick!" Kamal yelled out as he saw her come in view. "Or else!"

Simone's bare feet tip-toed closer and closer.

"Hurry the fuck up! I need help!" He barked another order out. "Ya little faggot boyfriend got a good hit off!" She was now towering over him not saying a word.

"Don't just stand there dumb bitch! Get me some help!" Simone stood still fuming with rage straight razor down at her side.

Kamal reached his hand out grabbing her leg with the last bit of strength he could muster up bringing her down to his level. "You gonna make me stump that ass again! Yours and Lil T! Now keep playing with me!"

Looking directly in Kamal's hate filled eyes, Simone knew that she had to avenge Joey's death. "I hate you and everything about you!" She finally blurted out raising the razor up to his throat.

"Bitch, I wish you would!" Kamal wasn't fazed keeping his fronts up, street style, to the end.

"You ain't shit Kamal! You deserve to die!"

"Come on Simone." He groaned in pain. "You's a weak ass little project tramp! Now get that motherfucker away from my throat before I make you eat that shit!"

Simone, for the first time ever, saw the heavy paternal resemblance of Kamal and Lil T. Their eyes were just alike, the thick braids, the barley noticeable mole that was on the left side of each ones lower jaw and the small dimple in their chin. Realizing those similarities made her hand tremble as she held the razor tight. "I hate you!"

Kamal got a last burst of energy putting one hand around Simone's neck making her dropped her weapon as she snatched back from his loose grip. "I knew you ain't have that shit in you!" He taunted pointing over at Joey's dead body. "You's a hoe like ole boy laying over there!"

An infuriated Simone crawled over in the corner of the living room grabbing Lil T's huge Sesame Street throw pillow. Aware of the screeching sounds of the police sirens closing in on her block and house, she rushed back over to a heartless cruel spirited Kamal who was fighting to live. Losing the bath towel along the way, a completely nude Simone closed her eyes shut and climbed onto him forcing the pillow down on his face. "I'll see your ass in hell motherfucker!" Her unorthodox retaliation was short but sweet. "Oh yeah by the way, for your information, back in the day, I fucked ya boy Big Ace twice! And trust, his dick was way bigger than yours!"

Kamal's arms flung wildly as Simone continued to maliciously cut off all means of his oxygen. Soon the demented ruthless street warrior's body gave in as his legs shook and his bowels totally released signaling that the Devil would soon have company. That much was destine. "Talk that bullshit now motherfucker!" Simone couldn't resist taunting Kamal, who of course couldn't hear a word that was being said as she bounced her weight on top of the pillow to make sure that she'd finished the job.

"You ain't so big and bad now is you? I thought so!" She answered her own question. "I hate ya yellow ass! I hate you with all my heart!"

Simone felt that she'd now settled the deadly score and vindicated her self on Joey's behalf. When she was a 100% sure that Kamal had taken his last breath on the planet Earth that she was made to occupy with him, she removed the sweat stained pillow and looked once again into Kamal's face. Just like Joey, Kamal's eyes were wide open seeming to be watching her every move. After hawking the hugest nastiest mucus filled glob of spit she could, dead into his eyes, Simone felt a slight bit of contentment watching it slide down the side of his face.

Hearing the sirens only houses away, the self appointed Death Angel tossed the pillow to the other side of the room and wasted no time in going back to her injured son's side who didn't move or make a sound as both of his fathers took their last breaths. He was innocent of everything that he was going through. He was just a pawn in his mother's game. Now the shit had hit the fan. It wasn't no come back from death. No turn around and no dang my bad.

Simone was still naked, but felt no disgrace. At this point none of that mattered. She held Lil T in her arms and rocked him back and forth praying to God for strength. "I'm sorry." She repeated with remorse. "I'm so sorry."

Within seconds a gang of police stormed the inside of Simone's house pistols in hand. The invasion of strange uniformed and plain clothes officers, in her front room, didn't make her blink an eye. Her battered still perfectly shaped nude body seemed to capture their attention, but she didn't care. Normally Simone would be full of wise cracks and insults for the police. This time was different as she was glad to see them coming.

"What happened in here Miss?" One cop inquired.

"Can you tell us who did this to you?" The next took his turn at trying to get an answer from a non-responsive Simone.

"Who are these two men?" A female officer asked while kindly grabbing the blanket off the couch wrapping it around Lil T and Simone in hopes of getting her fellow officers to show some respect.

Simone was in a horror movie and she was the star.

Chapter Twenty

"We got two males fatal and two wounded including a small child." The sergeant on duty called his shift commander informing him of the state of the crime scene as he waited on the ambulance to transport the victims. Simone's house was swarming with cops parading in and out of every room. Removing bullets out of walls, trying to investigate what went on, homicide detectives started to arrive and ask questions. As Simone, the local hood hero and Lil T were being brought out the house alive, Yvette and even fake ass Ms. Holmes shed tears of relief.

Simone refused to let Lil T out of her arms despite pleas from the EMS techs, who needed to check his vitals. "No don't touch my son!" She instructed in route to the same hospital she'd given birth at.

Looking down at a weary Lil T, she kissed his forehead whispering almost the same exact thing she did the day he was born into the game she forcefully manipulated him to become apart of. Simone was remorseful with her words. "Don't worry! We don't need no Nigga! I got us this time and we <u>still</u> ain't gonna want for shit! I promise you that!"

☼

Yvette and all the neighbors stayed posted in the same street that they'd just hours vacated from shame. It seemed to be some sort of a *Detroit Hood Tradition* to count how many body bags were brought out of a crime scene, like they thought a bloody hand would unzip the bag from the inside and jump out that bitch or better yet try their best to be the *All Star VIP Ghetto Fabulous Motherfucker* the local news cameras chose to put on *Breaking News*, that for real for real, really ain't know jack shit about what happened.

"That's what that uppity bitch get." One person coldly commented.

"Yeah. You right." A dopefiend put in his two cents.

"I wonder what the hell went on inside that house?"

"Who is in them bags?"

"Did she shoot they asses?"

"Why wasn't the baby moving?"

"Her tramp ass finally got caught in her shit!"

"Did yall hear all those gunshots?"

"I know Simone looked messy as hell!"

Person after person had their own speculation about the version of events and the way they could've unfolded. As the police made their rounds through the crowd trying to find any witnesses, Yvette was the only one who truly had something to say that could make a difference. Despite the disapproving frowns and whispers of folk who generally hated the police and considered helping them out *'Class A Snitching'*, even when it had to do with a neighbor, Yvette told them everything she'd seen from her bedroom window. Her information made it simple for the Detectives to easily establish a timeline of the deadly blood bath events of the night and exactly who Joey and Kamal were and what their affiliation was with Simone and Lil T.

With two smoking guns near each deceased body the investigation was sure to go smoothly, besides when Simone, a victim herself and a live witness, calmed down and dealt with Lil T's emergency situation, she could answer and clear up the entire homicide mystery.

Chapter Twenty One

It was almost the break of dawn and the sun was on its way to emerge out of the darkness. Richton Street was emptied of all the police, medical examiners and various news reporters that were camped out for hours trying to make heads or tails out of the blood bath inside of Simone's house.

Yvette sat on the edge of her bed watching out the window praying that Simone and Lil T were okay. None of the fancy cars, trucks or high price clothes she admired Simone for possessing really mattered at this point. After all, let's face facts. What good would any of that materialistic bullshit truly do if your ass was dead? Yvette wanted to call Simone's cell to check on them but as usual, Ms. Holmes was on the phone bad mouthing everyone she knew.
Of course, the main topic of discussion was Simone and the double homicide.

"Yes Sir ree. I couldn't believe it. That no good child done messed around and probably killed them boys."

"How do you know what happened?" The person responded. "They didn't arrest her did they?"

"Naw, but you know that don't mean nothing much these days and times. Don't you watch Cops or Court TV?" Ms. Holmes objected. "They probably gonna do it later, at the hospital."

"Let's stand in agreement and pray they don't." The caller requested. "Was the baby looking okay?"

Ms. Holmes raised her beige and red coffee mug to her old lips taking a small sip before answering.

"Oh My God!" The gossip queen yelled out testifying as if she was in the front pew of a down home country Baptist Church service. "Now you know I love me some Lil T, but I can't lie. He wasn't moving a single solitary muscle. The poor little thang."

"Oh no! Please don't say that."

"Yeah, but if he dies it ain't nobody's fault but that low life slut Simone. Matter of fact it would serve her right, especially after she put her dirty hands on me last night!"

"What did you just say?" The listener grew enraged.

"You heard me! Honey, you know good and damn well yourself she ain't worth two wooden nickels and never has been!"

"Regardless of what Simone is or isn't, it's certainly not your place to judge her, let alone speak out the side of your neck about the baby!"

"Wait one minute!" Ms. Holmes acted as if she had the nerve to be offended by being checked.

"Hell no! You wait one minute! I let you continuously talk about my flesh and blood last night and didn't stop you, but enough is enough! You're going too far!"

Simone's estranged now religiously devout mother periodically stayed in touch with her old running buddy to get updates on her daughter and grandson. But lately the last few times her and Ms. Holmes spoke there seemed to be an air of bitterness and contempt toward Simone. Even though there was bad blood, so to speak, between them, she would be less than a woman, Christian or not, if she let anyone say the type of foolishness that Ms. Holmes was trying to get away with.

"Oh…so now you want to play the mother role huh?"

"I don't have to try to do anything of the sort. I am that child's mother and Terrell is in deed my grandson whether I speak to her today, tomorrow or never."

"Whatever!" Ms. Holmes took another sip of her warm coffee. "Then instead of sitting on this phone throwing insults around, why isn't your self righteous behind down at the hospital?" Her sarcasms cut like a sharp knife. "Maybe I should be because it's painfully apparent that your only purpose in life is to be the devil's coconspirator!" With that being said Simone's mother angrily slammed down the receiver leaving a stunned Ms. Holmes looking completely dumbfounded. Whether or not Simone's mom actually went to the hospital, still remained to be seen, but at least hearing the tongue of a human form of a venomous snake wagging was over.

Meanwhile across town, Chari who was feeling guilty about the way she and Prayer treated Simone the night before, woke up and made it her first priority to go over to take breakfast to her home girl as a peace offering.

When she pulled up in front of the house Chari was beyond shocked. Yellow tape was everywhere and the picture window was shot out. The front door had a piece of plywood leaning up against it and the porch railing was dangling. A police cruiser was slowly driving by keeping a watchful eye on the house as well as old Mister Mc Nab, the block club president.

Chari frantically flagged the police car down, but got limited information from the rookie cop and his partner. Her head was spinning from disbelief.

With cell phone in hand, she immediately called Prayer who together with Drake who just made it in from his trip, rushed over. After talking to the next door neighbor, Mister Mc Nab, the trio found out some of what was supposed to have happened. The girls then quickly called a few hospitals finding out exactly where they'd taken Simone and Lil T. Prayer and Chari left to be by their friend's side while Drake got in touch with some of his folks so they could secure the house and the perimeter.

Mister Mc Nab was an elderly man and it was only so much he could do in the way of security. If Drake and his crew didn't damn near put steel boards, three pit bulls and an around the clock in house Negro, to watch that motherfucker, the crackheads and dopefiends would run havoc in Simone's crib. After a long tiring action packed night, the old man excused him self to lay down and take stock in exactly what his once calm, quiet, respectful and crime free block had been reduced to throughout the passing years.

As he waited for his boys to pull up, Drake grew infuriated at what had taken place. Looking at Joey's car and Kamal's truck, that were still sitting in the same place that the two deceased left them, made him make the final decision that Prayer was right. It was time to get out of the Dope Game for good and do something different and productive with his life.

When both young men, who Drake knew in passing, woke up yesterday morning neither had no clue that it would be their last day on earth. Each went to the park, hung out with friends, talked shit, partied, got they drink on and got some ass. But okay now what?... Now nothing! Ghost! Game over! Flat line! See you later, bye! Peace!

"This shit is definitely for the birds. Nigga's killing their own over dope and pussy!" Drake thought, cracking his knuckles taking a deep breath of the polluted city air. "After this bullshit, my girl ain't never hanging out with that foul bitch Simone again! I just hope that Lil T is all right. Lil Man done lost both his old dudes in one night! Ain't that some shit!"

Yvette was still looking out of the window and saw Chari pull up. By the time she finished throwing on some clothes and packing a bag, Prayer and Drake arrived. This was the time to prove her point, stand her ground and make a statement. She'd listened to Ms. Holmes run her mouth and talk shit for the last time. Finally realizing it was Simone's mother that her foster provider was talking to was the straw that snapped the camel's back. She was out that bitch! She'd make it on her own!

After hearing Ms. Holmes hang the phone up, Yvette made her presence known and felt. Shaking her head in disgust, she gave her, a swift smack to the face leaving her with some words of wisdom. "GROW THE FUCK UP!"

CHAPTER TWENTY TWO

☼

Prayer and Chari burst through the emergency doors of the hospital causing the security guards on post to become alerted. As the pair quickly approached the front desk, they practically knocked over a woman who was pushing a baby stroller. Without waiting in the line for the nurse on duty to call next, Chari blurted out her question. "Excuse me, but we're looking for Simone Harris!" Receiving stern glances from the people behind her didn't seem to bother Chari one bit. "She and her son were brought in here sometime late last night!"

Before getting a chance to respond, the heavy set Caucasian nurse was startled by the huge clanking sound of Prayer's keys slamming down on the counter. "Can you ladies please wait a moment?" The nurse pleaded as she shuffled through a stack of papers.

"This is an emergency!" Prayer insisted.

"Yeah this is an emergency!" Chari vouched.

"We all got emergencies!" A chick yelled out that was patiently standing in line coughing.

Chari turned around giving the female a look that could have set the bitch on fire. In order to put a stop to any drama jumping off, the nurse once again got Simone's first and last name. Pushing the information into the computer revealed the exact whereabouts of the girls injured friend and her son. With visitor's passes and directions, Chari and Prayer hurried to Intensive Care.

Upon exiting the elevator, they came face to face to a frazzled Simone with her black and blue bruised face pressed up against the window. She appeared done in as she held onto the frame to keep from falling to the ground. Simone's hair was all over her head and the side of her lip was busted.

"Simone! Simone!" Chari darted over to her friend's side. "We just found out!"

Simone made eye contact with Chari and Prayer then passed out. Them being in the hospital waiting room, her baby boy rushed into surgery, devoted Joey and criminal minded Kamal both dead on her living room floor was a combination that was powerful enough to knock a grown man on his ass.

"Quick, get her some water!" Prayer caught Simone in her arms and placed her in a chair. "There's a cooler over there." She pointed across the room.

"Okay, okay!" Chari filled two paper cones from the dispenser and carefully walked them over so as to not spill any. "Here you go."

Prayer took the water and splashed a little in Simone's face then shook her. A few moments later, Simone came around and burst out sobbing.

"We here girl! It's alright. Don't cry." Chari held her hand. "Where's Lil T? What did the doctors say?"

"Yeah have they said something yet?" Prayer added while handing Simone one of the cones of water.

After taking a small sip wetting her cracked lips Simone finally spoke. "I don't know nothing yet. They ain't telling a bitch shit! They just got me out here!" She leaned over in the chair from sharp excruciating pains that kept racing through her body. When she came in with Lil T, the nurses strongly suggested that she get checked out, but

Simone refuse medical treatment until she found out about her son's status.

"What's wrong?" Chari felt Simone's grip on her hand tighten. "Are you hurt bad?"

"I just can't believe it. Joey is dead!" She announced like Prayer and Chari didn't know. "Kamal killed him at my house. He gone yall! He gone!"

"We know girl." Prayer reached for Simone's other hand. "We know."

The friends, who were just hours earlier partying, sat in the room agonizing over Lil T's fate and mourning Joey for what seemed like hours before they got company from three people all at one time, the Surgeon, a Homicide Detective and a woman from Child Protection Services. By the grim expressions on all of their faces, the girls could only assume that what was about to come next would be nothing nice.

Prayer, Chari and especially the *Out 4 $elf* Simone, whom it would have an effect on the worst, braced up.

Chapter Twenty Three

A week later to the day that both of Lil T's possible fathers last walked the notorious streets of Detroit, they were simultaneously laid to rest.

"HE WAS LOVED!"

On the far west side of the city once known for Motown musical stars, a lucrative booming and stable automotive industry and of course the world famous Detroit Pistons a.k.a. The Bad Boys, Joey's double breasted Armani suit clad body was lying peaceful in a deep burgundy and silver top of the line casket. A solid 24 ct. gold chain with a cross was placed in one hand while his childhood bible graced the other. Drug dealer or not, Joey, along with his parents, never ever missed Sunday services where they were loyal and devoted members.

Florist as far away as Texas, North Carolina and Alaska had multiple deliveries to the funeral home that was handling the arrangements and the church, where the service would soon be held. Local youth groups, various organizations and the head Pastor were scheduled to speak and offer their heartfelt condolences.

As one o'clock neared, the tear filled inpatient crowd continuously grew. Joey's parents, per request of the church deacons, had to hire extra security to ensure calmness, inside and outside of the sacred sanctuary. Even though Joey wasn't a player when it came to the females, he was still loved and admired. It was more women in line than anyone else. Trevon and over twenty of Joey's close friends argued for days concerning who'd have the sorrowful distinguished honor of serving as pallbearers.

Even though Mr. and Mrs. Carter needed no financial assistance in the burial cost associated with their son, Trevon felt that considering their age and failing health he'd assume the organizing portion and all the running around that came with that. The Carters, who were devastated to lose their child, welcomed the help. The one and only thing they demanded be enforced was each and every security guard on post had a picture of Simone and would refuse her entry into the funeral services, even if it meant physically restraining her.

Too Joey's parents as well as the entire town of Detroit that'd saw the story on the news or read about it in the paper felt that Simone Harris was at fault for the tragic double murder at her house. Most newscasters and just plain ole folk used her as a prime example to the age old adage that *'playing both ends against the middle'* or *'burning the candle at both ends'* can only lead to getting ya' ass caught up in some serious bullshit and in this case death. If teenagers, confused females and so called grown ass women using their babies as human weapons to get back at the motherfucking men who refuse to step up to the plate and be fathers didn't learn a lesson from Simone, then so be it! That's on they dumb asses!

Long time residents of the *Murder Mitten* who'd lived through and witnessed the combination of the rise and fall of *The Young Boys Incorporated, The Chamber Brothers, Pony Down* and countless other high profile so called outlaws of their era, now ranked Simone up there when it came to coldness to the game of getting that dough. The fact that many believed she stood silently by watching Joey and Kamal shoot it out in front of her small innocent son didn't sit well with them.

Ms. Simone Harris, single mother, gold digger, back stabber and all 100% bitch was now labeled the new public enemy number one in Detroit.

Simone had already been made aware that her presence at Joey's funeral would be blocked so for once out of respect for someone other than herself and to avoid any type of disturbance, she didn't even try to show her still bruised face. Chari and Prayer promised her that as soon as it was over they'd bring her an obituary to the hospital where she was still posted with Lil T.

"HE WAS FEARED!"

The east side of Detroit was always known as straight gully. It was the side of town that most west siders dreaded venturing to. Smack dab in the middle of all the chaotic wildness that took place on Mack Avenue set a small dinky unattractive building. Bricks were missing out the front pillar. The paint was starting to peel and the awning across the doorway was damn near rusted out.

That was the home to Mc Matterson's Funeral Chapel. They were the cheapest route that a Detroiter could take to bury a supposed loved one. It also served as the facility that handled most State paid for services. Any unclaimed corpse, unidentifiable deceased individual or persons with no family or responsible party were their specialty.

Unfortunately for Kamal, he met one of those criteria's. Even though his boy, Big Ace, wanted to do right by him and lay him out in style, the police were still buzzing around asking a ton of questions pertaining the gun they'd found by Kamal's body that deadly night. Big Ace and the typically un-loyal crew weren't fools and opted not to put their freedom on the line by to much involvement. It seemed a few days after ballistics tests were performed on both weapons found at the crime scene, Kamal's was proven to have several bodies on it. *"Fuck that! Let the State bury that motherfucker!"* was the combine consensus of the entire crew, who could really care less if their reckless self appointed leader was dead. *"That stupid nigga brought that on his damn self! Beefing with that west side dude over a piece of rotten pussy!"*

After getting turned down flat trying to get the fellas to get Kamal some flowers, Big Ace sent the only floral arrangement that would be set next to the cheap low budget casket. As Big Ace cautiously drove up to the front door, he looked into the rear mirror for any signs of the police. Believing that it was safe, he parked and raised his still sore body out of the driver's seat tucking his gun in his waistband. He then pulled his shirt down to conceal it.

Making his way to the front door he noticed that the handle was welded back as he yanked on it. There was no one else in sight or waiting to pay their respects to Kamal, just him. Stepping inside Big Ace's nostrils took in the smell of stale mildew. You could tell it must have been some sort of a leak in the roof at one time or another and the owners never removed the musty carpet. Looking up at the 1960's velvet paintings that were on the wall made Big Ace think that Shaft was running that bitch!

Out of nowhere came a little old lady who appeared to be intoxicated. With a broom in her hands she used to balance herself and shoes on her feet that had definitely seen better days she spoke. "Yeah, you need some help?"

"I'm looking for my boy." Big Ace suspiciously sized the old broad up. "Yall supposed to have his body up in here somewhere."

"Ohh…" She slurred. "By the looks of you, you're probably talking about the youngster with all the holes in him. He's in there." Her boney finger directed.

Big Ace slowly walked into the dimly lit room and saw the lone flower on a pedestal next to Kamal just as promised. His blood started to boil as he saw how cheap the box was that these motherfuckers had the audacity to call a casket. Kamal's body was dressed in some old fashion Salvation Army throwback suit and his face was done up like a crackhead clown at a welfare kid's party. Big Ace wanted to go smack the cow shit outta who ever was in charge but at this point what good would it do? *"Damn Dude! They fucked you all around!"* was the only thing he could think of as he stood assumingly alone.

No more than five or six minutes of Big Ace somberly giving his road dogg Kamal a final face to face update on the crazy events that followed his untimely demise including the robbery that'd taken place out at the hotel, the devoted comrade heard a raspy cough come from the back corner of the dark room.

"Who dat?" Big Ace turned around placing his hand on his pistol. "Who back there?"

The shabbily dressed man almost immediately emerged out the shadow and into the light. Big Ace did a double take as dude came closer and his identity became apparent. Confused by his presence at the funeral home especially considering the way Kamal always disrespected and mistreated him, Big Ace started in on the questions.

"What the hell is you doing here ole timer?" He eased up the grip on his gun. "You the last cat I'd expect to see."

"I thought it was the least I could do." The guy coughed again this time trying to cover his mouth.

"What you mean? What you talking about?"

"I mean I know I wasn't shit in the way of a father figure, but Kamal was my son, my first born."

"Your son!" Big Ace yelled. "You Kamal's Pops?"

"Yeah." Willy Dale lowered his head in shame rubbing his unshaven face. "I thought you knew."

"Damn, is that why he used to be tripping on you?"

"I had it coming." Willy Dale reached inside the casket touching Kamal's chilly stiff hands that were peacefully folded. It was the last physical contact that he'd initiated since the day his young son knocked him out cold and struck out on his own. "Me and his mother was into some heavy shit back then when drugs were drugs, uncut!"

Big Ace still puzzled by what he was hearing let a remorseful Willy Dale continue without interruption.

"I'm just an old drunk now, but back in the day before Kamal's mother passed away, me and her got high off of everything we'd get our hands on. We was getting high the night he was born." He paused pondering the distant past. "It's a wonder he even lived a normal life with all the hardcore drugs she had flowing through her system."

Big Ace, for the first time since meeting Kamal, now fully understood what made his boy tick. It was now some sort of rhyme and reason to his bizarre behavior towards others especially his cruel treatment of women. *"Damn Dude, you really did have it rough."* Big Ace thought to him self as he and Willy Dale stood side by side paying their final respects. *"All you needed was some help."*

Chapter Twenty Four

☼

"GAME OVER"

It was shortly after four in the evening when Chari and Prayer showed up at the hospital still dressed in black. There they found Simone casually slumped over in a chair dead tired from exhaustion. The doctors had just wheeled Lil T out of the room from some more tests from a specialist that was called in to further evaluate his condition. In the week that'd flown by Lil T was still yet to regain consciousness. But nevertheless Simone was being a soldier doing her best to stick by her son's side. Barely closing her eyes and wearing the same outfit for two days at a time, the once young carefree mother was catching pure 198 degree hell. Whenever she thought the bad luck shit streak was ending, it was thrown back in her face.

Going through grueling countless interrogations from police authorities, an insulting and rude inquiry from Child Protective Services who challenged her parenting skills and with standing jeers of disgust and judgment from nurses and just about every individual she came in contact with who knew the story behind her son's injuries, Simone was at her wits end and about to go fucking nuts.

And if that wasn't enough turmoil for her to deal with, Simone, after being thoroughly checked out by an emergency physician on staff, found out the reason for her slight weight gain and constant vomiting. It seems that Simone was pregnant and had suffered a miscarriage. Even though the mental stress could've played a factor in her losing the baby, the doctor's examination proved that blunt force trauma to her bodies mid section and extensive damage to her internal female organs, thanks to Kamal's brutal act of rape with his grill, was the final determination.

Even though, once again, Simone had no idea which one, Joey or Kamal, was the father, it was still a sad situation and circumstance to lose a baby. And even worst than that, it was stated that nine out of ten times, Simone, who was just in the beginning prime of her life could probably never have children again.

☼

"Hey girl. How ya holding up?" Chari whispered with pity in her tone.

"I'm good." Simone tried perking up. "Just worn the fuck out."

"What's the latest with Lil T?" Prayer inquired eagerly hopeful that the situation had changed for the better.

"The doctors should be back any time now with an update from some uppity ass Negro they done flew in." Simone ungratefully hissed switching the subject. "Now tell me about Joey. How did he look? Was it crowded? Did yall bring me an obituary?"

Chari reluctantly dug in her purse to give Simone a few copies of thick picture filled expensively custom designed tributes to Joey Carter, one of her supposed to be baby daddies. What came next didn't surprise Prayer or Chari one bit. They knew the shit storm was coming and about to touch down as the two watched Simone look at and read the booklet cover to cover.

5, 4, 3, 2, 1 Bam!... "Son of a stankin' bitch!" Simone unjustifiably hit the roof. "Oh hell to the double naw!"

"Joey's old ass parents got a lot of nerve not putting Lil T's name on this shit! He's their only grandchild and they gonna just say fuck him! I knew I shoulda came to that bitch and turned the whole motherfucker out!" Simone was on a rampage screaming at the top of her lungs. "How they gonna play Joey's son? His ancient wrinkled face momma probably had that ugly ass broke down church going tramp, Belinda, he used to mess around with all up in the mix! I'm gonna stump that hoe! Please tell me that trick wasn't there! I swear to God if she was there it's gonna be some real shit!" Simone was out of control as she paced the floor. "I mean for real doe. How they gonna carry it? My baby should've been the first fucking name printed on this over priced piece of shit!"

Simone threw the obituaries against the wall as she stumped her feet and balled up her fist in anger. Prayer and Chari couldn't get a word in as their girl acted a straight fool. They stared at one another with amazement that after the fact that it was totally Simone's deceptive ass fault that their son's life was cut short, she still expected The Carters to list that child's name as a heir to their bloodline. As far as they were concerned if a DNA test revealed Terrell to be Joey's son, then by all means he'd be entitled and would receive everything that was coming to him.

"Calm down chick! Stop tripping on that. It ain't that important!" Prayer intervened.

"Just tell me what other bitches were there!" Simone questioned. "Who was crying and shit acting like Joey was they man?"

"What's wrong with you?" Prayer leaped to her feet shaking her head. "That boy is dead and gone and all you care about is who did what! You're pathetic!"

"Fuck you Prayer! Matter of fact! What ya snake ass doing here anyway?" Simone ran up on Prayer like she was about to swing. "Didn't you just throw me out your punk ass truck? And run over my damn shoe!"

"Bitch please!" Prayer smirked. "I wish you would! You think Kamal kicked that ass!"

"Come on yall! Don't start that mess up again." Luckily Chari was there to mediate. "Besides, Simone you can't behave like this in a hospital of all places!"

"Yes Miss." The team of doctor's returned with several charts in their hands. "I agree with your friend." One spoke up. "The level of your voice very much needs to be lowered and we'd greatly appreciate you not using profanity."

With no shame in her game at all, Simone rolled her eyes to the ceiling and poked out her lips. "Yeah alright then!" She was back to her old self. "Whatever!"

"Well that didn't take long." Chari thought. *"I knew the loving parent role was too good to be true."*

"Excuse me sir. How is Terrell?" Prayer asked the million dollar question. "What did your test reveal? Is he getting any better?"

Dr. Thomson with chart in hand looked at Simone for her approval to discuss her son's condition and the test results. When the defiant arrogant mother nonchalantly shrugged her shoulders indicating that she could care less what he said or who he said it in front of, Dr. Thomson delivered the final blow to end the game Simone started ever since Lil T's conception.

"I'm sorry Ms. Harris but your son Terrell…"

When he finished giving the present prognosis the room grew momentarily silent. It was as if you could hear the buzz of electricity pass through the air.

"WHAT IN THE FUCK DID YOU JUST SAY!" Simone went berserk. "WHAT DID YOU SAY!"

"I'm sorry Miss. We tried everything we could and still got no response from your son."

Chari and Prayer tried to get Simone to hear the doctor out and what he suggested she do in the weeks to come to aid Terrell in his long impending road to recovery, but Simone was not in the mood for hearing shit else. She'd heard enough. Karma had bit that ass! The once cocky fast talking gold digger who lived life on top of the world fell to the ground crying and mumbling the same word repeatedly. …….. "CRIPPLE!"

"CRIPPLE!"

"CRIPPLE!"

THE END

COMING SOON

Lil T does his thang!

His mother was a self-centered sack chasing slut.

His old dude was a psychotic deranged killer.

Most of Detroit would dread the day his parents laid down to conceive him.

His destiny was pre-determined.

His pedigree was official.

BASTARD SEED

By National Bestselling Author

MS. MICHEL MOORE

If you enjoyed this HOOD TALE, we hope that you'll read these other titles from Say U Promise Publications.

ESSENCE MAGAZINE BEST SELLERS

Say U Promise

Say U Promise... AGAIN!

Get It How Ya Live

Get It How Ya Live

"ONCE A DOPEFIEND, ALWAYS A DOPEFIEND! RECOVERY MY ASS! I'M TIRED OF THIS BULLSHIT!"

"Momma please! Momma, please wake up! Why you keep doing this stupid stuff all the time?"

Monica was screaming at the top of her young lungs as she violently grabbed her mother's frail sunken face slapping it repeatedly in an attempt to get her blood shot eyes to reopen and once again take in life. Like clock work, she then leaped to her feet and ran to get a cold wash cloth placing it on her mothers sweating forehead, causing her small framed body to slightly jerk from the shock of the fast sudden temperature change.

Everyone in the tiny apartment stood still, breath held, waiting for this week's possibly tragic outcome. Jenette was the center of attention once again.

"You won't be happy until your ass fucking die and leave us all alone!" She yelled while pounding on Jenette Howards' chest.

Normally, Monica never would have cursed at her mother, let alone raised her voice, but this was a special occasion. It was one of those all too famous, first of the month kinda special occasions that everyone in the hood waited and prayed for. Jenette had gotten her food stamps at 9:00 am that morning and instead of stocking the cabinets with even a few cans of soup or let alone, a tiny loaf of stale day old bread, she copped her usual choice of nourishment: DOPE.

Never once thinking about anything else but self, less than two hours later, surrounded by all three of her hungry kids, Jenette was laid the fuck out on the living room floor, damn near over dosing.

"Same shit, different day", Monica thought to herself as she went through the regular routine of bringing her mother out of her drug induced trance. The scary temptation was growing greater daily for Monica not to come to her mother's aid, with each passing episode of her bullshit antics.

Jenette was hood wide famous for over doing it. Whether it was a fifth of five o'clock gin and she was drunk passed out or her specialty, the needle left dangling in her arm after a good hit and would start bugging out going into convulsions. Monica didn't know which one she hated to witness more, her mother with too many drugs in her system or the days when Jenette was bold and busted, throwing up, scratching and gravely sick with the glare of a zombie in her eyes.

Under both circumstances, Monica was left to play nurse mate to her once loving mother. Jenette's hopeless search for love and acceptance led her to depend on anything she could get her boney hands on to try to escape the reality of her life. Her indulging in every drug known to man had torn her family apart and the sad part was, Jenette could care less.

Monica was the oldest of the three of Jenette's children. She was small for her age only standing, barely four feet tall. Her skin was dark bronze in complexion and her hair was brown, which matched her eyes.

She was a few months short of turning fifteen, but had the true knowledge of someone twice her age. Monica had no choice but to grow up quick considering that the odds were already stacked against her.

Like most of the other disadvantaged children in the economically stressed neighborhood they were forced to live in, Monica's mother was a 100% full pledged alcoholic junkie and proud of it. Day or night, Jenette could be found jumping in and out of cars trying to get that *'get high'* money which of course, left Monica to be both mother and father to her little sister and brother.

All three of the siblings had different sperm donor fathers that never came around or seemed to really give a shit about their kids well being. Jenette was heartless, seeming to take their absence out on her children. Life in Monica's small corner of the world was based on a lot of chaos and all out bullshit.

In between all the different tricks Jenette would have parading in and out of their small one bedroom apartment, to support her habit, Monica was fed the fuck up and left not knowing how much more of the confusion she could take. Instead of going to the movies, hanging out at the mall with friends or even trying to do her home work assignments, only one thing would fill Monica's long days… scheming to put food on the table and clothes on Dennis and Kayla's back.

The young girl couldn't help but think back to the first time her mother taught her to *'borrow stuff'* from the store. Jenette had her daughter stuffing steaks and pork chops down the back of her pants at an early age and running out of the grocery stores. When she'd be too sick to get out of the bed or off the floor, Jenette would even have Monica going to dope houses to cop for her. Sometimes she'd have to cook the shit up and shoot it into her own mother's thirsty veins. Monica was only the tender age of eight at the time it began, but her youth and innocence never mattered to her mother. That was life in the hood, at least Monica's.

****

Now ain't that some shit? And if that ain't enough foul crap to make you wanna smack fire out of Jenette's no good neglectful ass, then pick up a copy of...

GET IT HOW YA LIVE

...and really get pissed at the way alcohol and drug abuse can turn a mother against her own flesh and blood.

S.U.P. Publications
Submission Guidelines

To all interested Authors wanting to submit manuscripts for possible consideration. Please be aware and follow the below listed guidelines.

1. We request a brief but detailed synopsis.
2. The first four chapters are also required.
3. Double spaced, one side of page if possible, 12 point or greater.
4. Margins and semi-formatting.
5. No photo copies unless extremely clear and legible.
6. Please enclose all contact information, e-mail, phone, mailing address, etc.
7. Absolutely no electronic submissions. Mail to:

Say U Promise Publications

PO. Box 38162

Detroit, Michigan 48238

No Submissions Will Be Returned.

Please don't contact us for status updates.

We will be in touch in 30-60 days.

MS. MICHEL MOORE

MS. MICHEL MOORE

A self-published author, entrepreneur and motivator, **Ms. Michel Moore** has amazed an immeasurable audience with her aspiration and dedication to become the sole founder of **Say U Promise Publications** and an extremely talented Publisher having a keen eye for what the readers want.

Within a short stint of time, Michel has released four novels, including **Say U Promise** and its greatly anticipated sequel **Say U Promise Again**, which are both **Essence Magazine Bestsellers**, launched two highly successfully businesses; and currently has three pending novels on the near horizons.

In late spring of 2005 when opening **Hood Book Headquarters**, which boasts to have the widest readily available urban literature titles in the Metro Detroit area, Ms. Moore saw the need to offer *'her people'* another choice of knowledge expanding her hood success story opening, **Jayden's Joint**, which is ran by her daughter Tiffany Fletcher.

Ms. Michel Moore has dedicated herself in staying in her childhood home investing back into the community. From a tomboy jumping off garages with her brother Dwayne to being a West Side Cubs cheerleading coach, a respected business woman, parent, Detroit activist and of course **Essence Magazine Bestselling Author**, she has reached goals that once looked unattainable.

"I don't just write Urban Lit, I live it!"

OUT 4 $ELF

COMING SOON TITLES OF

2008

"Knowledge Cost"

"A HARD 7"

&

The third and final installment to the

Say U Promise

Trilogy

For details check out;
www.myspace.com/sayupromisebooks

MS. MICHEL MOORE

A HUGE THANK YOU GOES OUT TO EACH PERSON WHO PATRONIZES

HOOD BOOK HEADQUARTERS
313-515-7961

AN AFRICAN AMERICAN OWNED BUSINESS.

MS. MICHEL MOORE